"Is it the touching that's making you self-conscious?"

Liz figured she had two choices with this man: match his honesty or be intimidated by it.

"No, I'm getting used to that. It's your...body that's a little overwhelming. But then," she said dryly, "you know that."

He took a sip of his juice. "When you're an athlete, your body is simply a machine that you, your trainer and physical therapists push to go faster and farther. Any self-consciousness soon goes. But that's not your point, is it?" His gaze returned to hers, all male. "You're asking if I know women like my body. Yes, Mayor Light, I do." Luke smiled, but cynicism colored his next words. "But I also know it's not personal."

Liz squirmed in her seat. "It must be hell to be objectified," she managed.

His lips twitched. "Hell."

Dear Reader,

Finishing *Mr. Unforgettable* was a bittersweet experience because it meant saying goodbye to three guys I've been close to for years— Luke Carter, Jordan King and Christian Kelly. I've enjoyed writing about their friendship ever since they first threw punches in *Mr. Imperfect,* the book in which Luke Carter's marriage ended.

I always knew it would be a real challenge to come up with a woman strong enough for this wounded hero, but fortunately Liz Light marched onto the page, more than capable of taking Luke on.

In *Mr. Irresistible,* Kate Brogan revealed that Jordan King had taken other waifs and strays home during his youth, in addition to Christian and Luke. "A bunch of naughty boys and ratbags," she wrote in her testimonial, "who have grown up to be (mostly) responsible and law-abiding citizens."

They sound like perfect hero material to me.

So maybe this isn't goodbye, boys, but simply au revoir.

Karina Bliss
www.karinabliss.com

MR. UNFORGETTABLE
Karina Bliss

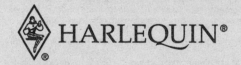

TORONTO • NEW YORK • LONDON
AMSTERDAM • PARIS • SYDNEY • HAMBURG
STOCKHOLM • ATHENS • TOKYO • MILAN • MADRID
PRAGUE • WARSAW • BUDAPEST • AUCKLAND

ISBN-13: 978-0-373-71475-9
ISBN-10:   0-373-71475-0

MR. UNFORGETTABLE

Printed in U.S.A.

ABOUT THE AUTHOR

Karina Bliss figured she was meant to be a writer when at age twelve she began writing character sketches of her classmates. But a scary birthday milestone had to pass before she understood that achieving a childhood dream required more commitment than "when I grow up I'm going to be." It took this New Zealand journalist—a Golden Heart and Clendon Award winner—five years of "seriously writing" to get a book contract, a process she says helped put childbirth into perspective.

She lives with her partner and their son north of Auckland. Visit her on the Web at www.karinabliss.com.

Books by Karina Bliss

HARLEQUIN SUPERROMANCE
1373—MR. IMPERFECT
1426—MR. IRRESISTIBLE

This book is dedicated to my writing family—
Abby Gaines, Sandra Hyde and Tessa Radley.
Not only can you gals spin straw into gold,
but you also teach me how to live.

CHAPTER ONE

SHE WAS IN BED with a man who wasn't her husband.

In the dark, the realization was slow in coming. Because this loving felt right Liz didn't question it, until she become aware—slowly—that the man whose mouth she devoured, whose body she explored, whose scent she inhaled, the man inside her, wasn't Harry but younger, stronger, bigger... and she didn't want him to stop.

She woke with a jolt and stumbled out of bed. Hands shaking, she fumbled with the catch on the French doors leading from the bedroom to the deck and shoved them open, needing air.

Her two-story house clung to Tuttle's Hill like a barnacle to a rock—which Tuttle's Hill was—a blustery outcrop hunched at one end of Beacon Bay, offering its clifftop inhabitants extensive vistas of the estuary from one side; the beach from the other. Liz and Harry had opted for estuary views, preferring the calm sweep of tidal river to the unpredictable and often wild Pacific.

But tonight the view couldn't soothe her. A hot sea breeze dragged at the sweat-drenched cotton of her nightdress as Liz raised her face to the crescent moon. "I'm sorry, Harry," she whispered brokenly. "I'm sorry."

Her husband had been dead for over two years and moving on was still so hard.

Oh, my love.

She wanted to be an old woman living peacefully with her memories, not thirty-five years old and betrayed by her body into needing a man.

Her nightdress lifted free of her body as it dried and Liz concentrated on her breathing, imagining the salty air dissolving the hard lump of pain inside her.

When she was calm, she walked back through the large, empty house to her study and flicked on the light. Her mayoral chains glittered from the desk where she'd dumped them, too tired to put them away.

She did that now, carefully straightening the twenty golden links so they lay flat in the velvet-lined box. Each previous mayor had donated a link and their names were engraved on the back.

Automatically her fingers traced the outline of

link nineteen, the district's most beloved mayor, tragically killed in a car accident in the middle of his third term. *Harry Light.*

Her own mayoral link was shiny and bright. The color of fool's gold, she thought ruefully, without the patina of age or experience. She shelved the box at the top of the wardrobe and reached for a report. *Wastewater-treatment upgrade options.*

Curling up in the big leather chair, Liz opened page one and looked at the chart. *Incidence of odor complaints within a one-kilometer radius of pump station over the past twelve months including weather variables.*

For a moment she was tempted to grab a pencil and doodle little creatures holding their noses around the margins. But her council staff and constituents wanted her to be dignified. Like Harry.

Frowning in concentration, Liz lost herself in the mysteries of pond desludging and trade waste bylaws until she fell asleep over her desk, dreaming about…

"Shit." Fastening the last buttons of his shirt, Luke Carter stared into the empty glove compartment of his 4WD. The tie was in his Audi S8.

He slammed the glove compartment shut, pulled on his socks and shoes and grabbed his briefcase. Nothing in it, but the town-planning department of Beacon Bay District Council appreciated the trappings.

The first time he'd visited the council offices he'd made the mistake of arriving in cargo shorts and a T-shirt, thinking he'd left the formalities of the business world behind him in Auckland.

His cool reception had quickly made Luke realize they expected the millionaire businessman, the former athlete. Hell, they wanted his Olympic-swimming medals dangling around his damn neck.

Over the following months he'd all but done it, too. Anything to get those po-faced, bureaucratic bastards off his back and signing off on Camp Chance. Actually, if they signed off on the camp, he'd *give* them the bloody medals.

Outside the car, the heat hit him like a blow. Still he shrugged on his suit jacket, muttering a curse as he caught sight of the elderly woman marching toward the council's entrance.

They met at the top step and exchanged smiles with all the ease of two gunfighters just before a trigger gets pulled.

"*Ms.* Jackson." Though she'd never let a man tell her what to do, Luke knew Delores hated the feminist honorific.

The faded blue eyes narrowed as she corrected him. "Miss."

"Of course, my apologies." He opened the door for her. "Here to snoop?"

Her majestic bosom swelled. "If you're bringing miscreants and delinquents into our community, we need to be assured that all the checks and balances are upheld."

"Here to snoop," he repeated. Dammit, the last thing he needed was the president of the Residents and Ratepayers Association finding a weakness.

They entered the blessed air-conditioned coolness of the council buildings on a waft of Delores's eau de lilac, a scent Luke had come to associate with bloody battle.

In the struggle to set up a holiday camp for under-privileged children on conservative Beacon Bay, this woman and her cohorts had cost the Triton Trust tens of thousands of dollars and months of delays.

Triton had won in appeals, but unfortunately many of the elderly population still equated the impending opening of Camp Chance with an invasion of the body snatchers.

If the place was ever bloody finished. "As always, Delores, a pleasure." Without waiting for a reply, Luke headed for the counter.

The council receptionist glanced at the clock. "The meeting's already started."

"My planner's there?"

"Ms. Newton arrived early."

Luke relaxed slightly. "Find me a tie, Mary, please. I'm desperate."

She folded her massive forearms. "What do you think I am, a magician?"

"Don't worry about the bunny."

Lips twitching, she waddled out back and returned with a luridly striped yellow-and-black tie. Luke's sartorial soul recoiled but he gave her a big smile as he put it on.

"You're a lifesaver."

A faint blush stained her cheeks. "Get in there," she growled. "You know they don't want to see your planning adviser. They want *you*."

They always wanted him. The elevator doors were closing as Luke reached them. He jammed his briefcase in the gap, and with a squeak of protest they reopened.

The mayor was the sole occupant. "I wondered why we were having trouble with these doors," she said dryly.

Luke stepped in. "Good morning, Your Worship."

"Ah! So, you're here as a supplicant." The doors

closed. In the confined space he detected a faint vanilla in her perfume, like everything else about the mayor, subtle and understated. As always, she looked cool and composed. Her long, ash-blond hair was pinned up, she wore a plain white shirt under a gray-blue silk suit, simply styled, but Luke knew good tailoring.

Both jacket and trousers followed her slim curves without accentuating them. Blue eyes would have completed the ice-maiden look, but hers were dark brown, the irises almost indistinguishable from the pupils. It made her very difficult to read.

He jabbed the button for the third floor. "I didn't see you at the site visit."

Though the lift was already moving, the mayor pushed the button again. "I'm sorry," she said. "Something came up. How did it go?"

The tour was intended to get former adversaries onside by being transparent and inclusive in the building process. "We didn't *quite* end up linking hands and singing 'We Are the World,'" said Luke, "but I'm starting to shake the image of big bad developer."

She smiled, and he added, "Any chance you're on the Resource Consents Hearing Panel?" Mayor

Light was one of the few people he respected on this council.

She was also oblivious to him as a male. Old or young, married or single, women had been flirting with Luke since his teens. The mayor was friendly, approachable and, for a beautiful woman in her mid-thirties, completely indifferent to the opposite sex. Still getting over the loss of her husband, Mary had confided when Luke mentioned it.

"Not my area," Liz said. "Councillors Bray and Maxwell are supporting the planning officer today." She ignored his snort, but he thought he detected a flicker of sympathy behind her fashionable black-rimmed glasses. "Why are you looking for consents when Camp Chance is near completion?"

Scowling, Luke punched the lift button to try to hurry it up. The council elevator moved as slowly as its officers did. "Your ecological adviser saw one skink during an inspection visit last month and slammed a moratorium on construction until we consulted an expert in herpetofauna."

She started to smile then realized he wasn't joking and adjusted her glasses. "Go on."

"The expert concluded the skink was probably passing through...they live in bush, not clearings, you see, something I tried to tell your so-called eco expert at the time." He paused, struggling to rein in his sarcasm. "So we're presenting his very expensive report and seeking permission to resume building."

"I see." Her serenity goaded him.

"Do you? If we're unsuccessful, the camp's opening will be delayed while we hunt nonexistent skinks and we'll be disappointing a lot of under-privileged kids."

Her expression didn't change. "I'm sure that will be taken into account in the decision." He couldn't imagine Elizabeth Light ever losing her composure. Even in bed.

Where the hell had *that* thought come from?

Luke loosened his tie. He was tired or he wouldn't be snapping at her. Up at six and at the building site, it was days like this he yearned for his old corporate life.

"Sorry…" He rubbed the back of his neck. "I didn't sleep much last night." He noticed she had faint smudges of exhaustion under her eyes, not quite covered by her expertly applied makeup. "Heat been keeping you awake, too?"

The mayor stared at him then a blush swept up her face until even the tips of her ears were red. She mumbled a reply then stared fixedly at the lights flicking between floors.

What the hell had he said?

She had a patrician nose, very straight, and he liked how her mouth tilted up at the corners…inherently optimistic. He hated defeated mouths, but the best his own could manage these days was a straight line.

The lift doors opened and, with a nod, she stepped out quickly. Three steps along the corridor she hesitated. "If things get sticky, remind them of Blue Heron Rise."

"That's it, just Blue Heron Rise?"

"No. Nice tie."

Luke looked down at the bumblebee stripes, then glanced up sharply, but the mayor was already walking briskly away. For the first time he noticed how high her heels were under the trouser hem.

Given that her council was predominantly made up of men, and bombastic ones at that, looking them in the eye had to be an advantage. The hint of vulnerability made her more human.

But what really intrigued him was that, for a moment in the lift, she'd been a woman looking at a man.

SNOWY PATTERSON was sitting in Liz's office, short legs planted in front of him, hands folded over a belly that testified to years of public-service functions.

"Did you know Resource Consents still has issues with Camp Chance?" Liz dumped her heavy briefcase on her mahogany desk with relief. "I just saw Luke Carter in the elevator." He'd inadvertently triggered a memory of her dream and she'd blushed like a teenager. Stupid.

"Yeah, poor bastard ticks off one condition of consent and another one jumps up to bite him in the bum." Snowy's farming background made for colorful colloquialisms, which he shared freely.

The deputy mayor's nickname sprang from the color of his hair, still impressively thick, even in his late fifties. His eyebrows jutted like tufts of snow-covered tussock over piercing blue eyes and a weathered complexion. "Political correctness gone mad if you ask me."

After nearly nine years in local government Snowy was also free to air his opinions of the bureaucratic process, a luxury Liz couldn't afford. "What is it now?" he asked. "Bush protection, items of historical significance on the site, breaching the earthworks allocation…the poor bugger's had them all."

"Skink capture and relocation," Liz explained and Snowy laughed until he cried.

"Anyone else would have given up," he said, "but all credit to them, these Triton blokes have hung in there. Not that you can walk away from million-dollar real estate, and God knows, with its history, it would be difficult to sell."

Luke Carter was one of three partners in one of New Zealand's leading tourism companies and Triton Holdings had bought the lot five years earlier with the intention of building a hotel.

Public outcry sunk the project and the land had sat idle, a convenient shortcut to the beach for locals, until the partners had sought approval to build a holiday camp for disadvantaged kids.

Despite opposition, this project had eventually won approval, largely thanks to Harry.

It was the only time Liz secretly opposed her husband's decision and it was the hardest of his causes to champion now. But she did it. "I told him to mention Blue Heron if he found himself stymied."

Snowy raised one brow. "It's not like you to be stirring the pot, you're usually taking it off the boil."

"The guy needs a break."

"He's not the only one, is he, Liz?" She glanced up from unpacking her briefcase to see him watching her. This man knew her too well.

Snowy pushed the *Beacon Bay Chronicle*

across the desk. "Delores Jackson threw her hat into the ring this morning." Local government elections were two and a half months away and nominations had only opened yesterday.

Looking at Delores's iron-gray curls and Special Forces smile, Liz's heart sank. Sure enough, the article was full of the geriatric militant's buzzwords—institutionalized corruption, conspiracy, vested interests—and what Delores intended doing about them.

Liz covered the newspaper with her sewage report. "I'd better officially register, then." She needed another term, not just to see Harry's projects to fruition, but to pursue her own.

"You've done a damn fine job, Liz. Harry would have been proud."

The rare compliment brought a lump to her throat. Snowy hadn't always liked her. Along with most of the district, he'd been aghast when his best mate and new mayor had fallen in love with a council clerk fifteen years his junior.

Harry hadn't cared but Liz did. She knew Harry was public property with his boundless energy, his dedication to the public good…and she was nobody, a migrant from the city.

She'd spent the five years of their marriage

trying to deserve Harry, winning over the doubters with her exemplary behavior. But she'd also built up a reserve between herself and other people.

Now she said awkwardly, "I couldn't have done it without your help."

He nodded. "You're ambivalent about standing again."

"Not ambivalent," she protested. "Tired. I've put in long hours this month, but I'm taking the afternoon off to babysit Harriet, so—"

"Before you make a final decision," he interrupted, "you should know I'm running against you."

CHAPTER TWO

THE AIR WHOOSHED OUT of her leather chair as Liz sat down. "Oh."

"Only my bloody prostate prevented me from standing last time." Snowy waited for a response but, still reeling at the news, she could only stare at him. "Dammit, I'm fond of you, Liz, but the mayoralty is a duty to you, whereas politics is my passion."

"Snowy, you have every right to run for mayor," she said quietly. "But so do I, that's the nature of democracy. And also speaking fondly, are you sure your health is up to this?"

"Yes," he said shortly, "so don't play the infirm card."

His mistrust stung but she wouldn't show it. "You know me better than that."

"You misunderstood me," he said gruffly. It was the closest Snowy ever came to an apology.

Liz struggled to be positive. "Well, at least two

friends can agree to a clean campaign, one that's issue driven with no personal attacks."

His laugh was a bellow. "Good God, nearly two years in the job and you still have illusions."

From under his bushy white eyebrows, Snowy regarded her with a mix of exasperation and affection. "I'm not going to attack you, Elizabeth, but I'm standing because I have attributes better suited to the job…experience, charisma—" she winced "—vision. And I'll be pointing that out. But I won't deny that you've done a great job as a caretaker."

She stiffened. "I didn't stand for the mayoralty to keep your seat warm." Was that why he'd wanted her to run? Because he'd perceived her as someone who'd be easy to displace?

"So you haven't been a councillor, so what?" he'd argued at the time. "You were working in local government when you met Harry and you were his mayoress for five years. People know and trust you."

Wily politician that he was, he'd then used the one argument that could sway her. "Otherwise, that right-wing bastard, Cully, will win by default and undo all Harry's good work." Liz had been swept to power on a wave of public grief and nostalgia for the district's favorite son. An easy victory followed by a heavy responsibility—filling Harry's shoes.

"Of course not," Snowy soothed her now, but he couldn't meet her eyes. "But you haven't initiated anything, have you?"

"Because I've been learning the ropes, riding shotgun on Harry's numerous projects. Although you know I'm advocating a new community center."

"Very worthy." For the first time his paternalism felt patronizing.

"Yes, it is. Dammit, a community needs a heart and that clapped-out hall hardly qualifies."

He reverted to his old impatience. "Without wanting to undermine your accomplishments, Liz, people elected you on Harry's reputation. Now the district needs a professional politician with a new vision. I mean this kindly—" his eyes took on a steely glint "—if you really want to protect his legacy, then quit while you're ahead."

He knew her fears and he was deliberately prodding every one. The realization saddened Liz, and made her decision easier.

"You're right about looking to the future." Snowy relaxed back into his chair. "I'll stand on my own merits."

"You'll get more votes under Harry's aegis," he

said bluntly. "And that's the last advice I'll give you. But you can't beat me."

He was probably right. "I have a heap of work to do," she said, smiling.

Disgruntled, Snowy heaved to his feet. "I won't announce my interest until tomorrow so you can reconsider overnight." He stopped at the door. "What would *Harry* want, Liz?"

"Probably to still be alive."

Snowy's face reddened. "Flippancy isn't appropriate."

"Neither is emotional blackmail." Liz kept her voice very steady. "Harry was too dear to both of us to be used as a political football."

When he'd gone, Liz took off her glasses and rubbed her eyes. She hadn't just lost a mentor, she'd lost one of her few friends.

And another link to Harry.

Pushing back her self-pity she tried to think rationally. Was Snowy a better person for the job? Kingpin of the old boys' network, his concerns reflected his interests—land management, sports clubs and business.

Services and facilities for young families, teens, the aged—these were areas he'd give lip service if he won.

Liz pulled out her diary and wrote *Reelection Priorities* then underscored it. Her most pressing need, now Snowy had deserted her, was finding a campaign manager. She wrote it down, added *Possible Candidates?* then chewed her pen. It had to be someone she trusted.

Ten minutes later her pad was still empty.

BLUE MOON? Blue gum? What the hell had the mayor said? Blue bird? Yes…it was a bird. While his independent planner, Caroline Newton, read her report to the Resource Consents Panel, Luke racked his brains. "Blue sparrow? Blue finch? Blue—"

Caro's knee nudged his, and he realized he was muttering aloud. Glancing at her statement, he saw she was only up to page twenty of twenty-five.

Why she still had to read it out loud when everyone had had the documents for a week was beyond him. He studied the three men who make a ruling.

Two of them had an elbow propped on the circular table and were supporting their heads with one hand, barely awake. Councillor Bray looked morc likc a basset hound than ever with his wrinkles pushed up around his deep-set eyes; fluorescent light flagged the bald spots in Councillor Maxwell's coiffed gray hair.

Only the council's new planning officer, John Dunn, looked as though he was following the proceedings, glancing up occasionally over his reading glasses and making notes in the margins. But it was the other two who worried Luke.

Bray's cousin owned one of the properties adjoining the camp. He'd appreciate any delays Bray could get him before "the hordes" as he disparagingly called them, arrived.

And Maxwell was a *NIMBY*. Said all the right things about helping the underprivileged but only associated with affluent retirees with low golf handicaps, and always voted Not In My Backyard.

Dammit, Luke needed every edge he could get. Blue tit…blue jay…his gaze settled on Delores Jackson, furiously scribbling notes in the observer gallery…blue bat…no, wrong species. At least she couldn't speak during this hearing.

As Caroline started reading page twenty-three, he drummed his fingers lightly on the table. For an athlete, long periods of inactivity felt like slow death. Still reading, Caro nudged his knee again and he stopped tapping. This time her warm thigh stayed pressed against his.

Casually, Luke broke contact. This wasn't the first time his planning adviser had signaled her interest, but the Beacon Bay population was too closely knit for transitory relationships, and since his failed marriage he wasn't interested in any other kind.

Caroline turned another page. Under the table, Luke's left foot started to tap. Celibacy had only intensified his restless energy. His gaze fell on the portraits lining the opposite wall and gravitated to Elizabeth Light's, one of only two women to hold the office of mayor.

She smiled directly into the camera but her eyes were remote. Yet in the elevator…

He wondered if the mayor missed sex now that her husband was dead, but decided no. Sex would have been a duty to such a restrained woman, something messy to be ticked off her list.

Idly, he scanned the row of pictures until he found her late husband. A good man, dignified and judicious, Harry Light had more than made up for rejecting the hotel project by his later support of the camp.

Luke tried to imagine Harry and Liz in bed together, then realized what he was doing and winced. Sorry, mate, rest in peace.

"In conclusion," said Caroline, "I ask that the moratorium on construction be lifted."

"Thank you, Ms. Newton." John Dunn took off his reading glasses. "We do have some questions for you and Mr. Carter."

Luke straightened in his chair. Let the games begin.

THE PHONE RANG as Liz hunched over her solid-oak desk, and she pushed her blank pad aside with relief. "Elizabeth Light speaking."

"Hi, it's Kirsty." The friendliness in her step-daughter's tone still thrilled Liz every time she heard it. "Just checking that nothing's come up to stop you from taking Harriet this afternoon."

"Are you kidding?" Liz stood and walked to the window, closing the Venetian blinds against the glare. "Nothing takes priority over that baby." She added wryly, "Not even a coup attempt."

"Ooh, that sounds interesting. Tell me what's happening in the world of paid work."

Liz hesitated. "Snowy's challenging for the mayoralty."

"But he's the one who made you run last time… Aaah!" Kirsty had inherited her father's political astuteness and prior to starting a family had worked in public relations. "Good old Uncle Snow," she said disgustedly. "Well, he won't be kissing *my* baby on the election trail. You're going to need one hell of a campaign to beat him." The fact that Kirsty gave her a chance of winning heartened Liz, until she added, "Who's your campaign manager?"

Liz picked up a paperweight. "I was going to ask you for recommendations…would any of your former colleagues be suitable?"

"Hmm," Kirsty intoned thoughtfully. "Actually I can think of someone. Dynamic, intelligent, politically aware, good experience in PR. Looking for a part-time job that would exercise a diaper-soggy mind."

"You?" Liz's brain started racing. "I didn't think you were ready to go back to work," she hedged. Their friendship was too new, too precious to risk losing, and campaign disagreements were inevitable.

Volatile and passionate, Kirsty had been nineteen when Liz married Harry, and had hated her relentlessly until the day he died. Kirsty had been Daddy's girl, a relationship that had grown even closer with her mother's death when Kirsty was fifteen.

Harry's marriage to a woman only nine years older than she was had been a profound shock, and nothing Liz did softened Kirsty's dislike. Ironically his death brought them together; no one else mourned his loss like they did.

"I'm worried about jeopardizing our friendship," she admitted at last.

"Lizzy, we're not friends."

"Oh." She dropped the paperweight.

"We're family."

LUKE CRUMPLED his notes, aware for the hundredth time that he had staked too much—personally and financially—on this damn project. "If you want to preach responsibility, gentlemen, maybe we should discuss council's negligence in not raising the skink issue earlier."

He paused, letting the threat of legal action wake everybody up.

Beside him, Caroline scribbled a hasty note and pushed it in front of him. *Don't antagonize!!!*

Screw it, he'd been listening to Bray and Maxwell paying lip service to environmentalism for thirty minutes. "This isn't about skinks anymore," he said. "It's about two—" with difficulty he stopped himself saying skunks "—councillors getting off on their power."

Bray's basset-hound eyes widened; Maxwell got

so red even his bald spots went pink. But the new guy, John Dunn, snorted, then covered his lapse with a cough. "I agree we've had enough discussion," he said. "The decision seems clear-cut to me."

"Well, it's not to me," Maxwell began.

"Hear, hear," Delores boomed from the public seats.

Luke raised his voice. "And let's not forget Blue—" please God, let this be it "—Heron Rise."

Dunn looked blank. "Blue Heron Rise?"

"Blue…Heron…Rise." Luke started to sweat.

Bray and Maxwell had their heads together whispering furiously; then Bray leaned over to Dunn, and muttered something behind his hand.

Caroline wrote, *I wish I'd thought of that!!!*

Maintaining his grave expression, Luke scrawled back, *I expect a discount!!!*

"It seems we're all in agreement." John Dunn had a twinkle in his eye. "Building resumes."

He walked down the stairs with Caroline and Luke afterward to avoid being ambushed by Delores Jackson, confirming Luke's opinion that Dunn was a smart man.

Turned out he was another Aucklander looking for a slower pace of life and, by his accent, which had a rougher edge when he wasn't officiating,

Luke guessed they hailed from similar neighbor-hoods. Dunn was effusive about the facilities Triton was now moving ahead with, less so about the future inmates.

"They'll trash the place."

"Careful." Luke put out a steadying hand. "Wouldn't want you tripping on that prejudice."

John looked at him blankly for a minute then reddened. "Sorry, mate, but—" his gaze swept over Luke's expensive suit "—you don't have any idea what you're taking on."

"Oh, I'll soon have them singing Gilbert and Sullivan and calling me sir." Luke opened the stair door, gallantly gestured Caroline and Dunn through into the council foyer. "And I'm looking forward to learning how to rap."

John looked at him closely. "You're having me on."

"I'm sorry." Losing his temper wouldn't help anybody. "Look, most of these kids aren't bad, just without choices or role models. And we're not expecting quick fixes. Every kid comes back to camp at least twice and there'll be follow-up schol-arships for those willing to take them."

Luke became aware that his voice was ringing through the foyer, and shut up. The other two were staring at him, embarrassed. God help me, he thought, I've become an evangelist.

"Your heart's in the right place, mate, but…" John's gaze slid over Luke's suit again. "I grew up around kids like that and they don't change."

"I *was* a kid like that. And I did change." Luke thrust out his hand. "Give them a chance, that's all I ask."

John shook it. "Chance. Guess that explains the name of the camp. Well, good on you for giving something back." With a nod to Caroline he turned toward his office.

"I never knew that about you." Her curiosity rescued Luke from painful memories.

With a shrug, he followed her out of the building. "It's not something I broadcast. But if it helps change prejudices, I guess I should use it." He looked down at the new permit in his hand, then kissed it. "Yeah, baby."

Caroline laughed. "Come over for a drink tonight to celebrate." Her invitation implied more than a drink and for a moment Luke was tempted, but these days moments were all he allowed himself. "Thanks, but I need to work."

"You know what they say about no play…"

"Makes Jack a dull boy. Yep, that's me."

Driving back to the building site to break the good news, he wondered if dull Jack was the same Jack who sat in a corner saying, "What a good boy am I!"

If it was, he reflected dryly, Horner had been misspelled.

THE HOUSE, when Luke got home midafternoon, was stifling from being closed up on a day when the beach shimmered in a haze of heat, and even Beacon Bay's white sand could scorch the soles of bare feet.

Opening all the doors and windows, he stripped to a pair of running shorts and a loose T-shirt, then leaped off his deck, down the sand dunes and onto the beach. It was too damn hot for a run but fitness was engrained in him so he picked up his stride, his trainers digging into the soft sand.

Besides, he'd be stuck in his home office all evening catching up on Triton business. While he'd delegated his day-to-day responsibilities in order to set up the camp, as a partner he still had a strategic role.

His property was at the less populated end of the three-kilometer beach, close to a tidal lagoon. But it took the length of the beach and back before Luke had run out the day's frustrations.

Panting, he walked the jelly out of his legs

alongside the green lagoon, with its shady overhang of gnarled pohutukawas.

Kids had recently created a deeper swimming hole by damming the sea end, but to counter protests from parents of toddlers they'd also formed a smaller, shallow pool between the sea and the sandbank.

On an incoming tide it made a perfect wading pool, but today only one mother—wearing a modest lime swimsuit, a big straw hat and sunglasses—stood knee deep supervising a blond baby.

In addition to wearing yellow water wings, the girl had a bright pink blow-up ring around her solid little middle and looked like the Michelin Man in drag. But she had a yummy mummy. Luke allowed his libido a quick scan.

A golden Labrador tore past him and thundered into the water with a joyful bark, sending spray over the woman, who yelped and then laughed. "Go home, Tolstoy, or I'll have you impounded," she warned and Luke realized he'd been admiring the mayor's shapely legs and beautifully rounded rear.

Tolstoy was a well-known sight on the beach; his elderly owner let the dog walk himself.

She turned back to the splashing baby, gently floating on the ripples over the sandbank and into the main lagoon. "Oh, shit!"

Luke grinned. So the mayor hid a great body and swore when she thought she was unobserved. The Lab swam to shore where it shook itself off in a whir of flying golden fur and raced up to Luke.

Giving him a cursory pat, Luke watched, amused, as the mayor gingerly waded in up to her armpits and grabbed for the baby, who floated just out of her reach.

Obviously, Her Worship didn't want to get her hair wet. As the baby drifted away from her, she made another grab and went under, her hat bobbing to the surface. Luke laughed until Liz's face broke free of the water and she tore off her sunglasses. She was terrified.

He exploded into motion, hit the water as the mayor went under for the second time, reaching her in three fast strokes, then hauled her, coughing and spluttering, into the shallows.

"Harriet," she gasped, all her attention on the child.

"She's fine." He retrieved the spinning tube with the splashing baby, the hat and the sunglasses. Liz grabbed Harriet, and the plastic squeaked under the pressure of her hug.

Rivulets of water streamed off her dark blond hair and down her face, splashing on the child, who began to whimper. With a shock, Luke realized the mayor was crying.

She thrust out the baby, and he took Harriet awkwardly and walked away, instinctively giving Liz privacy and himself space. The baby stopped fussing and stared at him with wondering eyes. He ventured a smile. The baby stared at his teeth.

"Can you talk?" he asked. The baby didn't answer. She was older than his goddaughter… Maybe two? He freed her from the inner tube and water wings conscious of the big brown eyes that traveled, fascinated, over his face. Now he understood the safety-gear overkill.

She seemed much younger and smaller without all her floaters, and he wished he'd kept them on.

"I'm sorry." Liz came over and took the kid from him. She looked pale. Barefoot, she was level with his shoulder. She tried to dry Harriet with a towel but her shaking hands made her clumsy. The baby's lower lip started to tremble.

Luke took Harriet back. "My house is nearby, let me make you a cup of tea."

As she hesitated, a group of beachgoers trudged into view, heading their way. Mayor Light jammed on her sunglasses. "Let's go."

CHAPTER THREE

BEACH BAG IN HAND, Liz followed Luke Carter up the dunes, focused on pulling herself together. Slowly, the shaking stopped and she became conscious of her wet swimsuit, her rat's-tail hair and the freckles on her nose, normally covered by makeup. *Of having fallen apart in front of a ratepayer.*

They stepped onto his deck, the same sun-bleached cedar as the two-story house. Most of the beach frontage was glass, currently reflecting the sand dunes, blue sky and a bedraggled woman. "You know," she said calmly, "I won't stay…if I could just refill Harriet's bottle with water?"

"I think your first task is more urgent than that." He handed her the baby and she nearly reeled at the smell.

"Oh!" The swimming nappy was supposed to be leakproof. Too late, Liz realized one tab had come loose. She held Harriet at arm's length and looked at the smear on her swimsuit. "Ugh!" To her dismay there was also a brown stain on Luke's sodden red T-shirt. "I'm *so* sorry…"

He followed the direction of her gaze and grimaced. "I wondered why the smell didn't go away." Gingerly hauling the wet T-shirt away from his body, he indicated a direction. "You two take the downstairs bathroom, I'll take upstairs."

The situation was so ridiculous Liz had to smile. "I haven't even thanked you yet."

He smiled back. It steadied the last jangle of her nerves. "A true knight errant wouldn't flinch from damsels who weren't potty trained. How old is your…your…?" She watched him try and work it out.

Harriet could be her child, Liz was young enough. For a moment she wanted that fiercely. "Step granddaughter," she said. "Fifteen months."

"Granddaughter," he repeated. "What are you, all of thirty-two, thirty-three?"

"Thirty-five." Being precious about your age was a waste of time when you were in public service. "How old are you?"

For a moment he looked surprised then grinned as he took her point. "Thirty-three."

It relieved Liz that he was younger. Made him

less dangerous, somehow. Holding Harriet well clear, she followed him through the open-plan kitchen/dining room to the bathroom and caught a better view of herself in the mirror.

"Oh!" Harriet gave her a beatific smile and pointed at her nappy. "Pooh," she said proudly.

Fifteen minutes later, Liz was naked when Luke nearly gave her a heart attack by tapping on the door. "You okay for towels?"

"Fine," she gasped, dragging one out of her bag. Then remembered the door was locked and relaxed.

"How do you have your tea?"

Harriet, now cleaned up and dressed, toddled to the door and reached up for the handle. "Out?" She looked expectantly at Liz.

"Wait for me, honey." Liz toweled down and reached for her underwear. "Milk, no sugar, please."

"I'll see what I can rustle up for the baby."

"Out," Harriet bellowed. The handle was low and her little fingers caught the edge. The nib-lock popped out and the door swung open. With a yelp, Liz dropped her bra and grabbed the towel, holding it against her front. Briefly her eyes met Luke's.

He turned his back, reaching one hand behind him to fumble for the handle. Harriet grabbed his fingers instead. "Juice," she demanded, and started leading him down the hall.

"Nice towel," he mentioned casually over his shoulder.

Liz shoved the door shut, turned back to the mirror and started rebuilding her shattered image.

THE MAYOR CAME into the kitchen while Luke and Harriet were staring into the fridge.

The mayor, not the woman. She'd pulled her wet hair into a French twist and covered her cute freckles with makeup. The ice-blue dress she wore was calf length and her heeled sandals matched perfectly.

"I gave her water," he said, "but she's hungry. Is there anything suitable for a baby in this fridge?" He looked again at the row of brightly colored sports drinks, the raw steak, a bar of chocolate and a small carton of long-life milk.

"That's kind of you," she said formally, picking Harriet up, "but I carry food." Out of the voluminous bag she produced a can of baby custard and a banana and sat with Harriet at the breakfast bar.

The baby ate it with lip-smacking relish while Luke finished making tea and brought Liz a mug. She avoided meeting his eyes. "Thank you."

Taking a stool next to her, he said curiously,

"How did you grow up in Beacon Bay and not learn to swim?"

For a moment he thought she'd deny it, then she sighed. "I'm not from around here."

"Auckland?"

Scraping banana custard off Harriet's chin, she didn't answer.

"I feel compelled to mention the mayoral swim-safe campaign."

"Ironic, isn't it?" She took off Harriet's bib and finally looked at him. "So now you know my terrible secret. The poster girl for water safety can't swim. It's an initiative I inherited."

He read the anxiety in her eyes. "I can keep secrets. Why don't you take lessons?"

"Because no one can see me learning. It would undermine the campaign." She put down a squirming Harriet who immediately toddled into the adjoining lounge toward a coffee table holding a crystal chess set. Liz caught her as she got there and turned her in another direction.

"This is lovely." She picked up a chess piece and caressed it with a tactile appreciation that surprised him. He didn't think of her as a sensual person. "It must be a joy to play with."

"I haven't had a game since I've been here." Too

few friends in Beacon Bay and none of them chess players. "You play?"

She put the knight down. "I used to."

Luke followed Harriet, who had her nose and palms pressed against the ranch slider that separated the western side of the lounge from a private courtyard. "Let me make sure this is locked, little lady. We don't want you falling in."

The baby stared beyond the glass to where the lap pool sparkled sky blue in a garden of hibiscus, palms and frangipani.

Retrieving Harriet, Liz asked, "What, the ocean isn't big enough?"

"A pool lets me swim year-round. Old habits die hard, I guess." He checked the catch on the ranch slider, but Harriet had already lost interest and had begun playing with the fine silver chain around Liz's neck.

"I saw you win the gold medal," the mayor said as they sat down again, "on TV. I was very proud to be a Kiwi that day." She misread his expression. "I'm sorry. You must get tired of being public property, having everyone claim a connection."

Smoothly he turned the subject. "You know how that feels, I imagine."

"I think your fan club's bigger."

"It was a long time ago." They weren't good days for him.

"People don't forget achievements like that," she said softly, and he realized she was thinking of her late husband. Tension uncoiled in his chest.

Harriet wandered off again. "I'll get her," he said, welcoming the interruption. "Finish your tea."

Left alone, Liz assessed her surroundings. Rimu floorboards gleamed red in the sun pouring through floor-to-ceiling windows to the east, but the lounge itself was barely furnished.

There were no cushions to soften the big leather couches, no artwork on the cream walls, no photographs on the fireplace mantel. It looked like the house of a man who had stripped his life down to its bare essentials.

So it surprised Liz when Luke reappeared carrying Harriet and a small basket of toys. "I bought them for my goddaughter to play with when her parents come to stay."

Liz looked at the eclectic selection, which ranged from rattles to sophisticated counting games. "How old is your goddaughter?"

He spanned his big hands, "About this big… sits, crawls, can't walk."

"Nine months to a year?"

"There you go."

She hid a smile and accepted the offer of a refill, knowing Harriet would squeal blue murder if Liz denied her a short play with the toys. And there'd been enough drama for one day. *No, don't think about it.*

Instead she focused on Luke, padding over to the kitchen to put the kettle on again. He wore a loose linen shirt, sleeves rolled up, over casual pants. Creamy white, they accentuated his tan.

She'd noticed Luke Carter's good looks before in the same incidental way she noticed the weather. Now it struck Liz what an extremely handsome man he was. With his damp dark hair sleek against his head, the perfect proportions of his strong cheekbones, straight nose and square jaw stood out.

He had a wide mouth, often quirked at one corner, and his eyes were an unusual light gray, piercing, yet giving little away. Idly she decided that women would find him very attractive, with his height and athletic build, radiating vitality and peak health.

She had a vague recollection that he'd been through a messy separation. The council gossip, Mary, would know the details if Liz cared to ask. But Liz wouldn't ask. Being in the public eye had only reinforced her belief that people's private lives were their business.

Her gaze returned to Harriet, busy gumming a red ball. The baby dropped it to pick up a rattle, her arm movement getting more and more frenzied with the joy of the resulting noise. Liz started to laugh with her. A sob caught in her throat, taking her by complete surprise.

If anything had happened to her…if Luke hadn't come along… Desperately she tried to hold the thoughts at bay but they kept coming. The next sob escaped. Jumping up, she headed blindly for the bathroom and almost collided with Luke.

"You're crying."

Liz kept her head down. "I have something in my eye."

Luke put down the mugs. "Let me see."

"It's gone, I think." She smiled brightly through the tears.

"Let me see." He tilted her chin while she blinked furiously. He gave her a gentle shake. "Breathe." She breathed, but that only vaporized her bravado. As Luke checked her eye, she tilted her head back farther but the brimming tears overflowed.

Desperately, she pushed his hand away. "I think I've cried it out—the thing."

"You don't have something in your eye, do you?"

Tears streamed down her face. She couldn't speak.

Luke drew her into his arms. "It's delayed shock—nothing to be ashamed of." His hug was light, friendly, unthreatening, but it was the first time a man had held Liz in over two years and she couldn't handle it.

"Please don't touch me."

Immediately he released her. "I didn't mean to frighten you."

She wiped away the tears. "You didn't…it's just…" How to explain the fear that came with bereavement, the shock of the new after the familiar.

"You don't like to be touched," he finished.

She nearly laughed. Touch was what she missed most, but not the comfort of strangers. Yet when she looked into his eyes, read his empathy, Luke didn't feel like a stranger. So she was honest with him. "I'm not used to being touched anymore," she said.

To her surprise he took her shaking hands, cradled them lightly between his. "Okay?"

She nodded. His warmth seeped into her fingers, her shaking eased to trembling, then stopped. "If I'd lost Harriet, too…" No, she wouldn't cry again. Liz broke contact. "I should never have taken her near the water. But I thought with the safety tube and staying in the shallows…" She straightened her shoulders. "No excuses."

"How about I teach you?" he suggested. "Swimming lessons for chess games."

"Oh, that's kind but…" She searched for a polite excuse. "My schedule is erratic."

He grinned. "Bring your chaperone if you like."

She shook her head vaguely. "I don't understand."

"You're feeling awkward because you think I've seen you naked—I haven't." *Only half-naked.* Fully concentrated on covering her front, the mayor had forgotten her back was reflected in the mirror.

Luke had turned away quickly but he could still summon an image of the long pale slope of her back, faintly pink from the sun, her apple-cheeked bottom and slender legs. But she didn't need to know that.

A blush tinged her cheeks. "You're very frank, aren't you?"

"I'm not a politician," he agreed. "You might find that refreshing."

She laughed. "*Being* a politician, I can't answer that."

"No pressure," he said. "Think about it." He almost regretted the impulsive offer already.

"I should get Harriet home."

His driveway opened to the cul-de-sac next to the public walkway to the lagoon, where Liz had parked her Ford sedan. Despite her protestations, Luke insisted on carrying the baby for her.

"Haven't you forgotten something, Mayor Light," he asked when she'd strapped Harriet into her safety seat and was ready to drive away.

Confused, Liz thanked him again effusively then started the engine.

Luke reached in the open driver's window to get her fake spectacles on the dashboard. He put them on, to confirm what he'd suspected over the past hour, then handed them back to her with a smile. "Like I said, I can keep secrets."

As she drove away, Liz decided she'd been wrong in her assessment. Luke Carter *was* dangerous. And she wouldn't pursue his acquaintance.

"AT LEAST WE NOW KNOW that Snowy's going to rely heavily on his experience as elder statesman." Kirsty leaned forward and topped up Liz's glass of chardonnay before she could protest. She'd been at council offices from dawn until seven; another glass would only put her to sleep. And she needed to concentrate.

Overnight, billboards supporting Snowy Patterson had sprung up like mushrooms in support-ers' backyards. Under his benign smile ran the slogan Wisdom, Experience and Vision. Vote Right, Vote for Patterson.

Liz and Kirsty had already met twice over the previous four days to thrash out her key policy points, but they were nowhere near ready to go public. Liz kicked off her shoes and sank back into Kirsty's couch. "Even more important to counter with my youth and energy."

Realizing she was massaging her aching feet with her free hand, she chuckled, nearly spilling her wine. She'd have to work on her youth and energy.

"I've already scored one coup." Kirsty's blue eyes, so like her father's, were neon with elation. "The Mayoral Swim-Safe Challenge for local schools is in seven weeks and traditionally the mayor fires the starter gun. Bo-o-oring!"

She swept back the fringe of her short black bob. "The coordinator was thrilled when I said you'll lead the swimmers into the water."

This time Liz did spill her wine. Dabbing the splotches on her white shirt with a cocktail napkin, she said nervously, "And when I'm knee deep I'll fire the starter gun, right?" Her heart sank when Kirsty sniggered.

"Keep that humor, it makes you seem more fun."

"I'd love to, Kirsty, but—" Liz seized the first excuse that came into her head "—I really don't have any time to train."

"You won't need to. It's only one hundred meters to the buoy and back. Look, I've already done a mock-up of the flyers."

She thrust one in front of Liz's face. Leading Light, the headline read.

Always ready to lead, Mayor Liz Light will be the first in the water in the annual Swim-Safe Challenge, which promotes swim skills to the district's schoolchildren. "All kids living on the coast should learn how to swim," said Mayor Light. "And it's our responsibility as adults to make sure they can."

There was a little cartoon graphic of Liz with her real head superimposed, bobbing in the water holding a life preserver. Liz started to feel seasick. "Any chance of that life buoy being on hand?"

She wondered if Luke Carter's phone number was listed while she mentally paced out the distance. One hundred meters didn't *seem* far.

Kirsty had already moved on. "I've looked at

your schedule over the coming weeks…there are so many opportunities, Lizzy, for showing vigor. Driving tractors with farmers, planting trees with the Forestry Service—"

"I'm also the incumbent, Kirsty, which means my first priority is doing my job," Liz interrupted. "And remember my primary platform is upgrading community services, not to mention enhancing the rural library serv—"

"Oh, lordy!" Kirsty rolled her eyes. "How are we going to sound bite *that*."

"A community is its people…all its people." Liz took a sip of her wine, warming to her subject. "And the district's profile is changing. We're no longer a population of—"

Kirsty groaned. "That's all very well but your first job is to get reelected. And to get the yes, you have to make it easy for voters to get a handle on you. Sex up your policies."

Liz laughed. "Is it possible to make local government interesting?"

"No," said Kirsty cheerfully, "so we'll simply work on you…. You look so much younger since you've started wearing contact lenses, by the way."

Liz stared at her fingernails. "Thanks."

"Snowy was right," Kirsty continued, "you

will get more votes by using Dad's reputation again, but—" she held up a hand when Liz opened her mouth to protest "—you're also right. This time around you've got to be perceived as your own woman."

"I *am* my own woman," said Liz quietly. She'd supported Harry's policies because she believed in them, even the one that was painful to her.

Absently, Kirsty scribbled on her pad. "Of course you are…. I've got it! How's this? 'Integrity and Inclusiveness. Vote Elizabeth Light.'"

Kirsty's husband, Neville, came into the room. "Bubs is finally asleep." He kissed the top of his wife's head. "You're very loud when you're excited."

She lifted her eyes from her notebook. "You don't usually complain." He laughed and kissed her again, this time on the lips.

Liz looked down at her hands, then straightened her wedding ring. She kept expecting to regain the weight she'd lost when Harry died but it hadn't happened. Maybe she should just get it made smaller.

"Speaking of love lives…" Neville poured himself a glass of wine and folded his lanky frame into an armchair. "Liz, remember Mark, the new accountant at my office who you met at our barbecue last weekend?"

"Yes, nice guy." He was a widower and they'd had a long chat about bereavement.

"He thinks you're hot and wants to take you to dinner. You interested?"

"Of course she's not," Kirsty answered. "God, Nev, you can be so insensitive sometimes."

"Can I?" Neville looked surprised, and Liz hid a smile. His volatile wife was usually the one who missed signals. Her gentle husband, on the other hand, saw too much. Only last week he'd told Liz she needed to get a social life. That was why she'd gone to their barbecue—to be social. Now she realized it had been a setup.

"It's too soon," Kirsty said, looking to Liz for confirmation.

But Neville spoke first. "It's been over two years."

Liz shifted uncomfortably on the couch. It sounded as if they'd discussed this before.

"You didn't know what a perfect marriage they had. Isn't that right, Lizzy?"

Neville snorted. "So perfect, you never accepted it while he was alive."

"I admit to being a spoilt brat who needed to grow up."

They glared at each other.

"Can I speak for myself?" Liz said mildly.

"She's right, Nev, I can never duplicate what I had with Harry. And as mayor," she added thoughtfully, "it's probably not appropriate to date just for sex."

Kirsty's mouth fell open; Neville grinned. Liz swirled the wine in her glass. "So tell Mark thanks, but no thanks." Kirsty immediately looked at Nev with an "I told you so" expression.

Her complacency annoyed Liz. It was her choice whether she slept alone, not Kirsty's. She still had a loving husband to keep her warm at night. Did her stepdaughter think celibacy was easy? Mischievously she added, "Harriet can get Nana Liz a vibrator for her birthday."

Maybe that's why she had the dream again that night.

As a punishment.

CHAPTER FOUR

IN THE END she had to hunt Luke Carter down. His phone number wasn't listed, and Liz knew if she left it until Monday when she could search council files, she'd chicken out, so she drove to his house the next morning.

He wasn't home.

She sat behind the wheel chewing her lower lip for a few minutes, then reluctantly drove to Camp Chance. To her relief there was a tradesman working on an outbuilding. He could get Luke for her. She didn't want to go inside.

As she picked her way over to him in heels more suited to the chambers of power than a construction site, Liz noticed the hammer hand was attached to one hell of a body.

Impatiently she swept some loose strands of hair up into her French twist, letting the sea breeze cool her damp nape, and told herself to settle down, wincing as her fingers brushed the bump on her head. She'd fallen out of bed trying to wake up.

Unfortunately the builder looked even better, closer. He stood on the scaffolding, clad in a pair of black shorts that clung to a shapely male ass, a leather tool belt and a pair of old trainers.

Liz made a mental note to talk to the building inspector. The man probably didn't even wear sunblock; his back was as bronzed as the cherub fountain in her garden.

But, oh, boy, was he built, his muscles slick with sweat from the summer humidity, his shoulders as broad and strong as the planks supporting him, and biceps that matched the bunching muscle in his thighs. No cherub this.

His shorts and tool belt sat low on narrow hips. As she approached, he swung around and she was reminded of a discus thrower, all twisting powerful grace. She lifted her gaze to meet silver eyes as cool as water and realized she was looking at Luke Carter.

"Mayor Light." He shoved his hammer into his tool belt. "Come for that personal tour?"

"No!" Still dazed, Liz realized she'd been too emphatic when he raised his brows. "I'm officiating at a citizenship ceremony this morning.

Shouldn't you have a shirt on?" *Silly thing to say.* "You don't want to burn."

"I'm in shade." He grinned. "Is that what you came to tell me?"

"No." She looked away. "I have to learn to swim one hundred meters in seven weeks. Can you teach me?"

"Probably not."

She glanced up again, too high, the sun above the roofline blinded her. "Okay then. Well, thanks anyway." Liz turned to go.

"And if you give up that easy, then definitely not." He swung himself down from the scaffolding. "Why the deadline?" While she told him, he reached for a drink bottle and drank deep, head thrown back, the muscles in his throat working.

She'd never thought of a man's neck as sensual, but it was strong, wide, dipping into a collarbone cut like seagulls' wings over broad pectorals and shoulders. He had the build of the 100- and 200-meter champion swimmer he was—a sprinter who relied on explosive power.

Luke squirted water over his head. Drops trickled down his brown neck, sparkled like diamonds in the smattering of hair on his torso. Liz swallowed and took a step back. "Sorry," he said. "Did I splash you?"

"Playing it safe. So, you don't think I can learn in seven weeks?"

"Are you frightened to put your head underwater?"

"Not if I can stand up."

"Can you float?"

"On my back."

"Are you stubborn?"

She lifted her chin. "I can do anything I set my mind to."

Keen gray eyes assessed her. "If I gave you two lessons a week and you practiced every day, you could probably do it. Have you got that sort of time?"

Liz gulped. "I'll make the time." Who needed sleep anyway? Sleep held dreams. Except… "But I can't ask you for that kind of time."

"I can manage two lessons, and I'll get a key cut so you can use the pool when I'm not around. It's shallow, so you should be okay alone. One half-hour swimming lesson followed by one half hour of chess. Deal?"

He held out his hand and she took it. She must have shaken it when she first met him, but Liz couldn't remember the warm, slightly callused firmness. "Why are you really doing this?"

"Blue Heron Rise. You helped me, I'll help you."

She smiled, and he saw a glint of mischief in her dark brown eyes. "It worked then?"

Luke wondered how he'd ever thought of this woman as cold. "Like a charm. Now what the hell is Blue Heron Rise?"

"A subdivision. About twelve years ago a developer successfully sued a council in the South Island for the costs associated with his project's delay. Councils think they've legislated out of liability, but it hasn't been tested in the courts yet. The specter of Blue Heron Rise can still rattle cages."

Luke remembered the councillors' faces and laughed. "Oh, it did."

"Now tell me why one of New Zealand's richest men is working with a hammer."

"The builders needed help one day when they were short-staffed and somehow this evolved into a permanent part-time job. And before you squeal on me to the building inspector, I supported myself through university as a builder's laborer." He wanted to see if the woman still lurked behind the mayoral facade, so he added innocently, "I've always been good with my hands."

Her expression didn't change, but she did swallow. "That doesn't explain why you're working on a Saturday."

He shrugged. "Working's pretty much all I've got to do in Beacon Bay. Most people are adopting a wait-and-see attitude about the camp—and me. The hotel project cast a long shadow." It was one of Triton's few failures and it still rankled his professional pride.

"Living in Beacon Bay," she said, "you must see the hotel wouldn't have worked."

"It's certainly a great place to pull up a rocking chair and a banjo," he said.

"Are you calling us backcountry hillbillies, Mr. Carter?"

"Wouldn't dream of it, Mayor Light…but change isn't always a bad thing. The hotel would have brought economic prosperity to the area. You can't tell me the town doesn't need it."

"We need it," she admitted, "but not at the cost of our beachfront character. Still, it doesn't matter now, does it? Everyone got what they wanted."

Not quite. "The camp exists on sufferance," he said. "When the kids who holiday here are accepted by the wider community I'll agree with you."

Something uneasy flashed in her eyes. She glanced down at her watch. "Duty calls. I have to go."

So the mayor's support wasn't unqualified? Now Luke was uneasy. But he said lightly, "So it's okay for you to work Saturday?"

"I don't have a life, either," she answered. "Oh, dear, I didn't mean to imply you don't have a life, just not here."

She was right, there was nothing to keep him here beyond the camp's opening, but the prospect of returning to corporate life in Auckland didn't thrill Luke, either. He'd pulled back from the business when his marriage broke up—to lick his wounds and reassess his priorities. The camp had filled the vacuum, satisfied a need to give back. After it opened, Luke didn't know what he wanted.

He shoved the thought aside. "Since we've established neither of us has a life outside work, what time do you finish? I'm heading up to Auckland tomorrow for business and will be gone a couple of days. A lesson will give you something to practice while I'm gone."

They made arrangements to meet at four.

"I'll park on the road so no one sees my car in your driveway."

With difficulty, Luke stopped himself from suggesting a secret knock. But his amusement faded as he watched the gentle sway of her hips under her pencil skirt as she walked back to her sedan.

Maybe he did have an ulterior motive, beyond repaying a favor and making allies in council. He missed the company of women who didn't have a relationship agenda. And unless he'd read the mayor wrong, the last thing she wanted to do was to jump his bones.

Thoughtfully, he put down his bottle. He'd *already* read her wrong once—she wasn't an ice queen, only a little frosty. And a touch of frost would feel pretty good on a day as hot as this.

Luke reached for his shirt. The mayor was right. He'd had too much sun.

LIZ THOUGHT she'd lost her fear of death when Harry died. But as the water closed around her, squeezing the last precious oxygen from her lungs, panic made her suck in instead of blow out. Chest heaving, she burst out of the swimming pool, coughing and spluttering for air.

Standing poolside in board shorts and T-shirt, Luke removed his sunglasses. "You told me you had no problem putting your head under."

Gasping, Liz fell forward on the sun-warmed

tiles edging the pool, needing terra firma. "I don't…usually." She loved the water, always had. On the rare occasions she'd visited the sea as a child, she'd gazed in envy at the kids splashing confidently in the shallows.

All that space, all that freedom. The ocean was what initially attracted her to move to Beacon Bay. But to deliberately empty her lungs, watch the air escape in tiny bubbles of life-giving oxygen…

"I could feel myself sinking and I panicked," she confessed. She'd expected to take to swimming like a duck to water. Not a lump of ballast.

"You will sink a little as you empty your lungs." Luke flicked through the book—Learn to Swim!—again. "Let's go back to floating, no exhaling." He grinned. "I haven't taught before so you're going to have to give me some leeway here. It's probably better if I get in the water."

He dumped the book and hauled the T-shirt over his head. Liz averted her eyes, but her heart thudded harder against the hot tiles.

Nothing to be ashamed of, she told herself, a body like that would raise a pulse in a dead woman. She'd been nervous about this ever since she'd seen him shirtless earlier. There was a splash as he dived into the water and she took the opportunity to adjust her lime swimsuit so it covered all her bottom. One of them needed to be decently covered.

Luke's dark head broke the surface, and the grin on his face suggested he'd seen her self-conscious gesture. Oh, God! Water streamed over the chiseled muscle of his shoulders and torso as he stood. Liz concentrated on his eyes, smoky-gray under wet black lashes.

"Okay. Float on your back like a starfish. If you start sinking, I'll catch you."

Slowly she leaned back, let the water hold her, then lifted her legs and tentatively stretched out her arms.

"Open your legs wider," he commanded. Liz bit her tongue to stop a hysterical giggle from escaping and started to sink. Immediately Luke's hand was under the small of her back. "Head back, muscles relaxed. Push your stomach up. The book says to pretend you're Santa Claus, all belly." He laid his other hand lightly on her abdomen and, startled, she tightened it. "No, Liz," he said patiently. "Out, not in."

She closed her eyes. Shutting him out helped.

"That's good. I'm taking my hands away now." Stomach up, head back, limbs relaxed—she could feel the difference. The afternoon sun was a caress through the cooling water.

Experimentally, Liz stretched out her fingers, became aware of her hair fanning out from her head. Opened her eyes to see Luke, a mountain of muscle above her, and sank.

"IS IT THE TOUCHING that's making you self-conscious?"

They'd stopped for a cold drink.

Liz figured she had two choices with this man. Match his honesty or be intimidated by it.

"No, I'm getting used to that. It's your…body that's a little overwhelming. But then," she added dryly, "you know that."

He sipped his juice. "When you're an athlete your body is simply a machine that you, your trainer and physical therapists push to go faster and farther. Any self-consciousness soon goes. But that's not your point, is it?" His gaze returned to hers, all male. "You're asking if I know women like my body. Yes, ma'am, I do." Luke smiled, but cynicism colored his next words. "But I also know it's not personal."

Liz squirmed in her seat. "It must be hell to be objectified," she managed to say.

His lips twitched. "Hell."

Amused, Luke watched her deciding how to respond. The mixture of curiosity and caution in her dark eyes reminded him of Harriet when he'd first picked the baby up. Flirt with me, he invited silently, you might like it.

Her eyes shied away. "Shall we get back to the lesson?"

Nope, innocuous flirting definitely wasn't part of the mayor's repertoire. Maybe he could throw in a couple of covert lessons. Obediently, he picked up the swim manual.

The irony of being an Olympic gold medalist looking at a primer on basic swimming strokes hadn't escaped him. But it seemed to have escaped Liz, who was looking at him impatiently, eager for her next instruction.

"Let's try a facedown starfish float," he suggested. "Don't bother about blowing bubbles this time. Just get comfortable lying with your face in the water."

He didn't laugh until she was semisubmerged and couldn't hear him. He was having fun.

His sense of superiority lasted until she started thrashing him at chess.

CHAPTER FIVE

A MONTH LATER, the gold wedding ring on Liz's finger caught the morning sun as she leaned forward in her deck chair, trying to hide her rising excitement. Hand poised above her intended target, she waited.

Only when Luke frowned as he awoke to his predicament did she slide her queen gently into position. "Check."

Across the chessboard his eyes met hers and her breath caught at the gleam of battle in those depths before it was obscured by a sweep of black lashes as he returned his attention to the game.

Luke leaned forward and dropped his forearms on the table that separated them, throwing the muscles of torso and arms into sharp relief. Throat suddenly dry, Liz reached for the dew-touched glass beside her and took a sip.

If anything, her physical awareness of him had

intensified, but fortunately she'd got better at hiding it. Her attraction to Harry had been cerebral. Luke's self-assured sexiness was potent and…distracting.

In the distance, the bells of Saint Aloysius called the faithful to Sunday mass and Liz felt the loss of all the things she'd stopped believing in after Harry died. Glancing at her watch, she saw it was barely 9:00 a.m.

With elections and the camp's trial run drawing closer, these sessions were usually jammed in at odd hours, but today they had the luxury of time.

Luke's hand crossed the board. A rook entered the fray—the king was safe. Not only safe, she noticed with dismay, but poised to counterattack. "Check," he said.

Glancing up, Liz caught the last flash of a grin and realized she'd been lulled into a false sense of security. "About time you made the game interesting," she said pleasantly.

Ice tumbled into her glass as Luke refilled it from the water jug. "You don't fool me."

That was a problem, Liz thought. Because she had to trust Luke in the water, she instinctively trusted him out of it. Except then he'd do or say something that reminded her of her first assessment. Dangerous.

"So when am I giving you a camp tour?"

Liz kept her gaze on the board. "Let me check my diary."

"Weren't you supposed to do that last week?"

Her queen took his. "What I love about chess," she said, "is that while the king's the most important piece on the board, the queen is the most powerful."

Luke tipped his glass for an ice cube, which he crunched between strong white teeth. "The queen may be powerful but she can't mate the opposing king without help." He took her knight. "Speaking of allies, how's the election campaign going?"

"Bray and Maxwell have thrown their weight behind Snowy."

"They're like two pilot fish trying to avoid being eaten by a great white shark."

Liz laughed. "If you're trying to distract me, it won't work." She moved her bishop to cut off the black king's last means of retreat.

"I'm the one who needs to concentrate." Luke bent forward over the board and she took the opportunity to study him, a smile hovering on her lips. Their growing friendship had been an unexpected bonus.

The man needed a shave. His rugged jaw was shadowed with a weekend's growth. Tendrils of black hair, sun-dried after an earlier sea swim, stirred in the warm breeze and his eyebrows were touched white with sea salt.

She experienced a sudden shocking urge to push his sun-warmed body into the chair and kiss that firm mouth until it softened under hers. To run her hands down the taut muscle of his shoulders and—

His gaze suddenly lifted to hers and awareness tightened between them like a bow. No, she thought dazedly. No, that's impossible. Missing sex was one thing, doing something about it… She wasn't ready. Reaching up for the sunglasses on her head, she slipped them down to hide her confusion.

Luke's biceps stretched taut as he leaned back and rested an arm across the back of his chair. "I think we have a stalemate."

LUKE COULD TELL by the blush staining the mayor's cheeks that she knew he wasn't talking about chess.

But Liz wasn't ready to discuss their growing attraction. "We'll call it a draw, then." Retying her crimson sarong more firmly around her bathing suit, she stood up, barely glancing at her wrist before she said, "Goodness, is that the time?"

"You took your watch off to go swimming," he reminded her.

All credit to the mayor; she rallied. "My inner clock tells me when it's time to go."

Lazily, Luke pushed to his feet. "Aren't you lucky to be so attuned to your body." Her startled gaze shot to his and he smiled innocently. Oh yeah, he recognized the signs of someone desperate to get laid. He'd lived with them for months.

The nervous energy, the almost obsessive focus on training in the search for physical exhaustion. Liz's build was naturally athletic, and he could already see swim-specific toning in her arms and legs, a tightening in her glutes. Hell, who was he kidding?

The mayor had always been desirable, but her disinterest had made his interest academic. Luke didn't need to chase women; they chased him. But for some reason Sleeping Beauty was stirring— he'd felt the heat of her gaze on his body—and he wanted to be the guy who kissed the reluctant princess awake.

Their swimming lessons had become a torture. Every time Liz bent over to pick up her towel he knew exactly where her tan would change to creamy white across her bottom. A glimpse of her cleavage and his mouth went dry. He felt like a teenage boy in the throes of first lust—but was far better at hiding it.

Unlike Liz, who seemed to be in a permanent state of shock at finding herself prey to such base desires. Her naïveté turned him on, made him want to take her to bed and find out what else shocked her.

When she'd left he returned their glasses to the kitchen, then opened the dining-room doors to the sea deck.

The only movement on the dunes leading down to the beach was the swaying of spiky, cotton-tailed grasses in the early sea breeze. It would grow with the heat of the day until by midafter-noon it shook them like rattles.

Since regaining his single status, Luke's sexual encounters might have scratched an itch, but that was all. He'd been married a long time and casual sex didn't sit well with him. He liked Liz and he was hot for her—a friendship with benefits seemed the obvious next step. Both of them needed to safe-guard their public images in Beacon Bay, which meant any affair had to be conducted discreetly, with someone they could trust.

And that was the problem. Luke didn't entirely trust her.

Elizabeth Light made time for things that were important to her—like these swimming lessons—and could recite her appointment schedule for the next month. Yet every time he suggested a tour of the camp, she made up some excuse or pretended she'd forgotten. It contradicted her public support, made him suspicious.

But there was another, more important reason. She'd brought Harriet to lessons with her a couple of times and he'd seen how much she loved that baby. She probably wanted another husband, one to father the children she'd never had with Harry. Luke wasn't that man.

Since his separation, Luke counted the cost of every liaison with a woman, and this one was priced too high. With a sigh of resignation, he reached for his running shoes.

LIZ WAS SO TIRED she forgot to turn her mobile phone off during an afternoon council meeting and the theme tune to *Rocky I* interrupted Councilor Bray's monologue on item nine—approving security cameras on the council building to discourage graffiti.

The tinny melody rang out again. Those who recognized the tune started to laugh. With arms that ached from daily swimming practice, Liz fumbled through her bag, silently cursing her campaign manager.

Kirsty had insisted on reprogramming the phone's ring tone to encourage Liz to think like a winner. Feeling like a complete idiot, Liz switched it off, but not before she saw Luke's number flash up. "Sorry about that," she murmured, then took advantage of the interruption. "And thank you, Councillor Bray, for that useful summary on modern youth."

"But I haven't fin—"

With the ease of long practice, she cut him short, restated the notice of motion and took a vote. "Surveillance cameras approved. Meeting closed—" she glanced at the clock above the portrait of the queen "—at 2:55 p.m." As soon as she got the chance, Liz stepped into the corridor and returned Luke's call.

"Liz, I have to cancel our session today."

The stress in his voice was almost palpable as they rescheduled for nine-thirty the following night.

"Is everything okay?"

"No," he said bluntly. "Most of my staff has gone home with food poisoning. Social Services' final inspection is tomorrow and we're nowhere near ready." She didn't have to see him to know that he was pacing.

"Call for volunteers."

"I've put the word out, but too many locals are still ambivalent about this facility."

They weren't the only ones. Liz's hand grew clammy on the phone. All she had to do was say goodbye, hang up. But she'd never been any good at looking the other way. "I'll come," she croaked, "for a couple of hours."

"Thanks." With that casual acceptance, he rang off. See, Liz reassured herself, it's no big deal. But she clasped one hand around her other wrist like a frightened child. You're an adult now, she reminded herself, deal with it.

Back in the boardroom, Snowy canvassed for more allies. With elections less than a month away, Liz was falling behind in public-opinion polls because, as a frustrated Kirsty kept pointing out, she kept doing her job instead of schmoozing like everyone else.

"Excuse me," she said. The others stopped talking and looked around, Snowy impatiently.

Liz relayed Luke's predicament and asked for volunteers.

"I've got council business to attend to," Maxwell said. Only an hour earlier she'd heard him book a tee at the local golf club. Others immediately seized his excuse.

"I completely understand. Of course, council business takes priority over self-promotion."

Snowy's gaze sharpened. "What are you talking about?"

"The *Beacon Bay Chronicle* showing us all pitching in, getting the camp ready for the underprivileged kiddies." Liz picked up her briefcase. "But if you're too—"

"The *Chronicle's* doing a story?" Maxwell interrupted. He smoothed his comb-over.

She crossed her fingers behind her back. "It's a suggestion." Which she'd make as soon as she had the privacy to call the editor.

Everyone suddenly found a reason to leave immediately until only Snowy lingered.

"Why would you share the glory…I can't figure it out." Their relationship had deteriorated over recent weeks.

"That's because my motives are pure," Liz said sweetly.

"Look deeper," he suggested.

Stopping for gas on the way to camp, Liz damned Snowy's acuity. Morally, it was the right thing to support the camp, but only her friendship with Luke had pushed her into confronting her phobia.

And, heaven help her, not all her thoughts of that man were pure.

Pulling out her cell phone, Liz dialed the editor

of the *Beacon Bay Chronicle*, and for the second time that day crossed her fingers. A third-generation family business, the newspaper was so firmly entrenched that no rival had ever survived. The monopoly allowed the Swann owners to operate according to their own idiosyncratic code.

The current editor, Josephine Swann, was a thirty-year-old Katherine Hepburn. "I won't stab you in the back," she'd told Liz at their first interview. "I always attack from the front." Liz had a couple of scars to remind her never to mistake their mutual regard for friendship.

Fortunately Jo loved the idea of photographing politicians doing manual labor.

"I need a new angle for the weekly electoral countdown," she said. "Incidentally, you do realize that you're the only politician who hasn't been hounding me for coverage? Does that mean you're confident of winning?"

"Oh, no, you don't. I'm not giving you any reason to use the headline Mayor Declares Competition Sucks."

Jo laughed. "You're getting too clever for me. See you there."

"Make it as late as you can, will you? Let's get some work out of them first."

While she waited for her gas tank to fill, Liz washed the sedan's windscreen, trying to distract herself from the impending ordeal.

"Beth?"

She dropped the squeegee back into the water bucket and turned around automatically. And found herself looking at a stranger, a tall, slim brunette in cutoff shorts and a baggy pink T-shirt.

Then the name the woman had used registered and she hid her shock under a polite smile.

"I'm sorry…. What did you call me?"

"Beth…Beth Sloane." Doubt entered the woman's voice. "It is you, isn't it?"

Her childhood name… Liz opened her mouth to agree. "No," she said instead. "If I look familiar it's probably because you've seen me on election billboards. I'm Elizabeth Light, the mayor."

"That could be it." Liz tried not to flinch as the woman's curious gaze lingered on her face. "The likeness is amazing."

"Really?" Liz turned back to her car and replaced the petrol cap. She'd been expecting this day for years; now it had come, she couldn't deal with it. "I get that all the time. Apparently I have doubles in Bluff, Christchurch, Hamilton…." She rattled off a few more towns and cities, nowhere near Auckland. "Does nothing for the ego I can tell you." Shock made her ramble; she'd finally recognized this woman. "You're passing through?" she asked as casually as she could. *Please God, be passing through.*

"No, my husband and I just moved here. I'm Rosie Cormack, by the way."

Reluctantly, Liz took the woman's outstretched hand, hoping her childhood acquaintance wouldn't notice her cold fingers. "Welcome to Beacon Bay, Rosie. So what brings you to our neck of the woods?" *Tell me you're isolated on a dairy farm somewhere.*

"I'm a counselor at Camp Chance. Though today I'm a de facto decorator." Ruefully, Rosie scraped at a paint spot on her T-shirt. "I've been picking up extra paintbrushes in town."

"Camp Chance," Liz repeated. It was the last thing she expected.

Wariness came into Rosie's eyes. Obviously she'd already met a few detractors. "That's right… well, I should be getting back. Luke's waiting on these."

It was the perfect moment to say, "I'm heading there myself, so see you soon." Or take a deep breath and admit, "Rosie, I am Beth Sloane… Light is my married name." But Liz didn't. Couldn't.

Instead she said goodbye, paid for her petrol, got back into her car and fastened her seat belt. And sat. Deeply ashamed...and relieved she'd gotten away with it.

A horn tooted behind her, reminding her to move. Starting up the engine she pulled forward into the car park and picked up her cell phone. The incident had proved one thing. She wasn't ready for the camp. With trembling hands, Liz sent Luke a text message.

Sorry, can't make it. But the cavalry is coming.

At home, she dropped her keys on the polished mahogany hall table, then hesitated. From the lounge the mantle clock chimed the hour with silvery bells, the sound trembling through the house.

Coward.

Liz climbed the stairs to her bedroom, dominated by the dark, intricately carved four-poster. She'd lightened its solemnity with white silk-and-satin bolsters, crisp Egyptian-cotton sheets, the bed overhung with billows of snowy chiffon.

Her princess bed, Harry had called it, completely at odds with the rest of their furniture, which was classic comfortable.

When he'd died she'd forced herself to clear

his books, his clothes, his golf clubs…determined not to make a shrine to him. But she'd kept one thing. Opening her closet, Liz pushed aside her power suits.

Her fingers closed on merino wool and she pulled out Harry's favorite sweater, the faded, misshapen garment he used to haul on for winter gardening, the one she'd always nagged him to throw out.

I just need a little more time.

Her grip tightened as she buried her face in it and breathed deeply.

Sometimes if she tried really, really hard she could still evoke the faint smell of wood smoke, the light astringency of his aftershave, perhaps even a whisper of warmth.

She stood there a long time but today, it didn't happen.

"Dammit, I'm driving down."

"In your Ferrari, I suppose?" Mobile phone pressed between ear and shoulder, Luke picked up his spanner and tightened the bolts on the bunk he was assembling in one of the new dorms. "Yep, that'll make the locals feel like helping out the poor little rich boys."

"Fine," Christian said grudgingly. "I'll borrow

Kezia's car." Despite his predicament, Luke grinned. His partner's wife insisted on driving a station wagon, a newer model than the one she'd once pursued Christian in, but still affectionately derided by her husband as an H.O.S…heap of shit.

"We've been over this. I'm the ex-foster kid who got us into this. You're the guy in the black hat." Christian Kelly had spearheaded the original hotel proposal that had generated such heated opposition.

"Then I'll ask Jord to fly back from Sydney to—"

"What? Come be diplomatic and unobtrusive?" Months earlier, the *Beacon Bay Chronicle* had raised concerns about Jordan King's fitness to be a camp trustee after a respected columnist questioned his ethics. Though the disparaging story had been disproved—and Jordan was shortly to marry the journalist—they'd decided it was politic for him to stay away until the camp opened. "Besides, you two need to keep earning the big bucks to pay for this."

They'd been naive about the level of sponsorship the camp would attract and were way over their original budget.

Luke hesitated before he added, "If the camp doesn't get new sponsors soon—"

"I'll tell the tobacco companies we'll put a cigar

in every kid's welcome pack," Christian finished for him. "One problem at a time, buddy. Right now, I'll organize a crew of friends and relatives to come down and help."

"Uh-uh. Not until we've exhausted local options," Luke insisted. "I don't want to perpetuate the 'them and us' mentality."

His friend gave an exasperated sigh. "I don't like this, Luke. You're taking on too much alone. We're all in this together, remember?"

"Yeah, mate, this is temporary."

"How many months have you been saying that?"

"I'll keep you posted," Luke promised and hung up.

Christian switched off his mobile and, frowning, looked across his wide veranda toward the blue sky over the flat, golden fields. If the Ferrari was out, then Luke definitely wouldn't approve of the helicopter.

He heard his wife's footsteps on the wooden deck, then she wrapped her arms around his waist and leaned her cheek against his back.

"You're worried about him, aren't you?"

Feeling her warmth, some of Christian's tension dissipated. "Maybe it's the sensible thing to stay away, but it's almost as if he doesn't want us there."

One hundred meters down to his left, a duck came to land in the pond, webbed feet skidding across the surface of the water. The golden willows he and Kez had planted around it last autumn barely lent shade to the waterfowl hunkered under it.

"His reasons are sound, aren't they?"

"Yeah, but…" Staring over their land, Christian tried to articulate his growing sense of disquiet. "He's working too hard and he's alone too much. His Auckland visits are getting fewer and they're all about Triton business or the camp trust. When was the last time he came to stay here? Or the last time he, Jordan and I played pool and talked shit in a bar?" Kezia said nothing, a sure sign she had a theory.

Christian turned and cupped her face. "Okay, out with it."

Her golden-brown eyes widened. "It's a busy time with the camp, things will settle down."

"I'm waiting."

"Isn't his divorce final this month?"

"My God, has it been two years already? But what's that got to do with anything? After what Amanda did to him, he'll be painting the town red."

She pushed a strand of long hair behind her ear. "You and I are playing happy families, Jordan's about to get married…"

"Which is exactly why we've been trying to fix Luke up lately."

"I don't know if you and Jord are the best— Hey!"

Christian, relieved, had dropped his hands to her sweet ass and squeezed. "It's not easy," he admitted. "Luke has some cockeyed notion he's better off alone."

Kez gave him her old schoolteacher look but didn't remove his hands from her butt. "Huh. Where have I heard that cockeyed notion before?"

He pulled her closer, nuzzled her soft, dark hair. She smelled of rosemary and redemption. "The most fervent saint is always a reformed sinner."

"I didn't reform you," she protested. "You corrupted me."

His hold tightened. "So how about showing me what you learned before Maddie wakes up from her afternoon nap?"

He expected her to say no, they were in the middle of revising a new business plan for their other baby, the Waterview Hotel, and papers were spread across the dining room.

Instead she whispered huskily in his ear, "Clear the table."

CHAPTER SIX

LIZ'S CANCELLATION annoyed Luke. But his disappointment annoyed him more.

He hadn't anticipated her offer of help, but he'd been ridiculously pleased and—okay—relieved when she'd made it. He didn't like the niggle of doubt he felt every time Liz made an excuse not to visit camp. Luke liked her; he wanted that to be uncomplicated. Because if it was uncomplicated he might reconsider acting on their attraction.

He looked at her text message again. The cavalry? What the hell did that mean?

Shoving the cell phone back in his tool belt, he positioned the new bunk and hauled over another assembly kit, trying not to think about the twenty-five bunks still boxed in the other dorm.

Rosie stuck her head around the door. "I picked up the extra brushes…any more recruits arrive?"

"Delores Jackson." He knew she was there to snoop, but he'd decided beggars couldn't be choosers. She was supposed to be cleaning windows, but last time he'd checked he'd found her inspecting one of the storerooms. Unrepentant, she'd commented, "Four-ply toilet paper—no wonder you're over budget."

He'd probably kill her before the day was over.

"And unfortunately," he added, "we also lost another couple of staff to the bad steak pie." Thank God he hadn't been here for lunch or he'd be sick as well. Now it was all down to him and the vegetarians.

Rosie's face fell. "Rats, that cancels out the two I recruited in town."

One step forward, three steps back. Luke feigned cheerfulness. "More will show up."

Her expression told him she didn't buy the Little Miss Sunshine act, either. "I'd better get back to painting." At the door, she paused. "Do you know Mayor Light very well?"

As well as she wants me to. Luke laid out the frame of another bunk. "Yeah, she's one of us." *I think.*

He meant a camp supporter but realized they were talking at cross-purposes when Rosie frowned. "That's surprising. I got the impression she'd been keeping her past a secret."

Intrigued, Luke put down the pieces of wood. "You know her?"

"Yeah. She almost talked me out of it but Beth always had this gesture when she was nervous and trying not to show it—"

"Beth?"

"Elizabeth. We called her Beth."

Beth…Elizabeth…Liz. "Go on."

"She grips one hand at the wrist with the other. Like this." Rose showed him and Luke recognized the gesture. Liz had used it a lot since she'd realized she was attracted to him. "What do you mean, 'she nearly talked you out of it'?"

"She pretended she didn't know me."

"Okay, now I'm really confused. *How* do you know her?"

Her brow wrinkled in puzzlement. "You said you knew she was one of us?"

Understanding finally dawned. "You mean…"

"Yes. She and I were in a foster home together."

Councillor Bray stuck his head in the door. "Where do you want us?" As Luke stared at him, he added impatiently, "Come on, man, we haven't got all day."

AT NINE the next evening, Liz sat in her car in Luke's driveway, engine idling, and considered her options. There weren't any.

She had to learn to swim—Kirsty had snowballed the event into a major fund-raiser for schools. All the kids were getting sponsors and a local radio station was putting up ten dollars for every meter Liz swam. Reluctantly she turned off the ignition and got her kit from the trunk.

But did Luke still want to teach her?

Or was he another in a long line of people she'd disappointed by not showing up yesterday.

That morning Snowy had beamed benevolently from the front page of the *Chronicle*, his white hair haloed by the sun streaming in the window behind him as he made the camp beds. Snowy and the Seventy Duvets was the headline.

Kirsty was furious. "'Altruistic mayoral candidate, Snowy Patterson'…bullshit! Where the hell were you?"

"I wasn't feeling well, I had to go home."

Kirsty had immediately apologized. "Sorry, but it's not fair. You did all the organizing and Snowy takes all the credit."

Others weren't so understanding.

"You looked well enough when you were asking

for volunteers," Maxwell had said acidly. He'd been photographed with a toilet brush and wasn't happy.

Liz's allies on council had also felt let down. "Even if you'd taken a couple of painkillers, showed your face for half an hour and *then* gone home," Susan Blackmore had confided in the cafeteria. "Snowy won some serious brownie points by default."

It had been a hard day, bracketed by two sleepless nights, but the worst was still ahead. Steeling herself, Liz knocked on the door.

"It's open," Luke called. She found him in the pool, a splashing shape in the deep twilight. A wash of lazy jazz spilled out of the speakers. "Mind putting the pool lights on?"

Liz flicked the switch and the water shimmered into viridescent relief. Cast into shadow, his expression was impossible to read. "Thought I'd get some training in while I waited. Come on in."

"Oh. Sure." Self-consciously, Liz slipped off the tracksuit covering her lime bathing suit. Should she mention yesterday first? As she hesitated, her left foot caught in the pants and she grabbed the back of a deck chair.

"Are you too tired for this, Liz?"

God, yes, to the bone. "No, I'm fine…you?"

"I've always been a night owl. It's the early mornings that kill me."

She stepped down into the bright water, barely cooler than the sultry summer night. In one corner of the courtyard, a shrub bloomed among the tropical plants. *Cestrum nocturnum*, Queen of the Night, its small, trumpet-shaped white flowers only released their heady perfume after dark.

Luke picked up the flutter board at the pool's edge and green light stippled the broken surface of the water and dappled his pectorals.

"Today's lesson is about trust."

Liz sank a little lower in the water. Mentally, morally and politically she supported the camp but emotionally she was a traitor.

Luke tossed the flutter board aside. "Trusting yourself. I want you to do torpedoes—arms stretched out in front, kicking and holding your breath—without using a board."

"But that's going backward." Using the flutter board, she'd already advanced to turning her head to the side and taking big breaths. The next stage was adding the arm movements she'd been practicing independently. The book said so. "Losing the flutter board comes last, surely?"

"Think of this as a confidence check."

"My confidence is fine."

"You always look confident," he agreed. "But we won't know for sure until we take away the buoyancy aid. And I'd rather test that now while we still have time to make adjustments."

"I'm…sorry I didn't make it yesterday by the way." There, she'd said it.

"Hey, you more than did your part. Councillor Maxwell told me you were the recruiting officer. Of course, he was complaining about you not showing up, but later I heard you weren't feeling well." His voice was very gentle. "Sure you're okay now?"

She hadn't been sick and didn't deserve his sympathy. "I'm fine," she said abruptly. "Let's do this."

The water rippled as Luke moved closer. In the luminous green half light his irises were a shifting, shimmering gray.

"When you're ready."

She took a deep breath and launched herself forward, her fingers automatically grappling for the board and not finding it. In a panic she stopped kicking and stood up. "I'm sinking."

"You're not."

Liz tried again. Again the fear sent her stumbling to the surface after a few kicks. Breathing hard, she faced him. "This is ridiculous. I still need the flutter board."

"Not for this, you don't."

What did he want from her, this man? Didn't he know how hard she tried? Didn't everybody know how hard she bloody tried? "This isn't building my confidence, it's undermining it," she snapped. "We only have five lessons and two weeks of daily swimming practice to get this right."

"And you're doing really well," he soothed. "All credit to you, Liz, I didn't think you could do it. You're a gutsy woman."

"Damn right I am. You think this is easy?"

She was near tears and didn't know why. He was being so kind. And then suddenly she did know why. Liz got out of the pool, wrapped herself in a towel.

"Rosie told you, didn't she? Who I was."

Who I *was*? That bothered Luke. Why was this woman disowning a past that only made her achievements more impressive? "Yes."

She looked down at him, her expression cool. Her pale hair, darkened to the color of wet sand, dripped water over her tense bare shoulders and made splotches on the burgundy towel.

"If you want details, you're going to be disappointed," she said crisply. "I don't discuss my childhood."

Yesterday he might have called her withdrawal coldness. "Did Harry know?"

The temperature plummeted below zero. "He respected my decision not to talk about it."

A mistake, Luke thought, but kept that opinion to himself. "You know we have a similar background?" He'd shared a sanitized version with Jo Swann of the *Beacon Bay Chronicle* yesterday and the article had appeared next to the picture of Saint Snowy.

"Yes, I read it." Her lip curled. "Maybe I should do the same, it might win me a few pity votes."

"That was my motivation," he said evenly. "Might as well screw some benefit from a shitty childhood."

Liz stumbled to a chair and sat down. "I'm sorry. I don't know what came over me."

"What have you been telling people all these years?"

"Only child, both parents dead... Adopt a tragic expression and they back off pretty quickly."

Now he understood her ambivalence about the camp—it was a skeleton on her doorstep. "No wonder you never accepted an invitation to visit."

But she wasn't listening. "Who else has Rosie told?"

"No one."

She lifted her chin. "I'm a private person and I want to stay that way. No pity votes."

"Rosie won't tell anyone else." He lifted himself to sit at the side of the pool, feet dangling in the water. "You know, Camp Chance is very different from the institutions we grew up in. Let me show you, Liz."

But she was already shaking her head. "You deal with the past your way," she said. "I'll deal with it in mine. And I choose to forget."

"But you don't forget," he said softly. "Do you?"

She clasped her wrist. "Can we get back to the swimming lesson now?"

"Of course." Luke let the subject drop.

Liz got into the pool and started practicing with a terrified determination that was painful to watch. Knowing better than to interfere, he made comments where necessary, occasionally jumping in to correct her body position, mostly sitting on the side, watching her.

Beth had kept to herself, Rosie had said. One of those kids who got noticed by being quiet, being good. Luke had been a troublemaker himself—it had certainly got him attention, too. The wrong kind. His thoughts became bleak, so he refocused on Liz, who was readying herself for another torpedo.

Already too slim, she'd lost another couple of pounds, due more, he suspected, to a punishing schedule than daily swim practice. He made a mental note to buy some energy bars...get some food into her.

She got to the other end and stood up, turned to him relieved. "I did it."

"I think we should increase the lessons to three times a week." Making the deadline would be touch-and-go, but if anyone could do it, Liz could.

When he hauled her out of the water, she kept hold of his hand. "Are we back on track?" she said. Luke knew what she was really asking.

Her breasts were still heaving from her recent exertion, the nipples clearly outlined under the wet Lycra. Luke picked up her towel and wrapped her in it. She needed a friend more than she needed a lover. "Yeah, Liz, we're back on track."

She stiffened. "I don't want your pity, either."

"That's good because this chess game is a decider and I have no intention of going easy on you."

"You want to play *now?*"

They needed to normalize their relationship, so

he ignored the dark circles under her eyes, the sway of exhaustion. "That's our deal, isn't it?"

A ghost of a smile touched her lips. "I'll get dressed."

THE PHONE RANG while he was setting up the board. Luke glanced at the clock. Ten-fifteen. Only one person called at this time of night.

"Hey, Jord, welcome back."

"What's this bullshit about not wanting our help?"

"So how was the food…the in-flight movie?"

"We're coming down in the morning…and no arguments."

Luke stopped teasing. "I don't need you…it's sorted. Social Services approved the facility this afternoon." It occurred to him that organizing volunteers was the second kindness the mayor had done him in her quiet way. He resisted favors…the obligation they implied; yet she kept sneaking under the radar.

"So the trial run can go ahead as planned?"

"Yeah, fifty kids arrive Sunday…right about the time you touch down in the Cooks Islands as a married man."

That gave Jordan pause. "Wow," he said. "You're right. I've been so damn busy with work

and wedding preparations, it hadn't registered."
Another silence.

"Luke?"

"Yeah, buddy?"

"The thought doesn't scare me. Tell me I haven't grown up."

Nostalgia bit deep. "Okay," he said, "I won't tell you." The first time Luke had seen Jordan, he'd been doing chin-ups over a ceiling joist in a student bar—eighteen years old, cocky, wild and good-humored. Luke's swimmer's shoulders had won him that contest, but Jordan had wasted him in the drinking game that followed it.

"Kate's refusing to see me this week… She's had this 'no sex' policy in place for a fortnight… some bridal-torture thing."

"My heart bleeds for you," said Luke. "You know how long it's been for me?"

"Hey, Christian and I have been trying to set you up with a good woman…you keep turning them down."

"That's because I don't want a good woman, I want a bad one. Introduce me to all the commitment-phobic hotties you used to date."

"I've ruined them for other men. Seriously, Kate has this amazing friend—"

"Jord, you and Christian have got to let this matchmaking mania go. It's driving me crazy."

"Okay, I was saving this as a last resort…but you know my sister has always had a crush on you."

"I'm going to hang up now."

"No, wait." The banter went out of Jordan's voice. "You're alone too much these days, we're concerned you're turning into a hermit."

"No, I'm not." Impatiently Luke turned away from the window, saw Liz sitting in front of the chess set. How long had she been there? "As a matter of fact, I've got company—female company—right now."

"Blow-up dolls don't count."

He handed the phone to Liz. "Do me a favor and say hello to my partner Jordan.

Gingerly, Liz took the phone. "Hello?"

A male voice said, "Well, I'll be damned."

"Sorry to hear that." It occurred to her that this guy could be useful. "Say, do you know Luke's weaknesses in chess?"

"Well, yeah, he always—"

Luke wrenched the phone from her grasp. "Oh, no you don't." He walked into the kitchen with the phone. Smiling, Liz finished laying out the chess pieces.

"No, we're not sleeping together," she heard him say in a low voice and tried to concentrate on her first move. "She's a friend who happens to be a girl…a difficult concept for you, I know." He came back and handed her a chocolate bar. "Her name?"

He looked down at Liz, a question in his eyes. Unwrapping the bar, she shook her head. "Frederica." He winked at her. "Fred for short. What does she look like?" The twinkle in his eyes became a spark. "Brown eyes, blond." His expression tightened and he turned away. "Yeah, I know I swore off blondes after Amanda, but like I said we're just friends…. Fine, don't believe—" He stopped. "Hang on a second, Jord?"

Putting his hand over the receiver, he turned back to Liz. "Ignore everything I'm about to say."

He took his hand away. "No pulling the wool over your eyes, is there, mate? Yep, that's the reason I haven't been spending weekends in Auckland the past couple of months…too soon to say if it's serious. Listen, I was thinking of bringing her to the wedding…"

Liz choked on her chocolate and he waved a reassuring hand.

"So don't you and Christian go fixing me up with anyone, will you? She's got a jealous streak…

Uh-huh. Okay, well, she's waiting for me in bed, so I have to go…oh, the chess?"

He looked at Liz and shrugged as much as to say, might as well be hung for a sheep as a lamb. "It's a kinky game we play. Remind me to tell you and Kate the rules sometime. Your sex life's gonna need spicing up when you're an old married couple… Uh-huh, I love you, too… See you Friday night at the stag."

He rang off. "Don't panic, I'm not expecting you to." For an unreal moment Liz pictured bed and kinky chess, then realized Luke was talking about the wedding. He sat down at the board. "But this will stop them from lining up Ms. Rights on the day."

"You're not interested?"

"God, no. The only relationships I have with women now are strictly platonic." He paused to make his move. "Or strictly sex."

Liz stiffened in her chair as he stretched a hand toward her. Casually, Luke snapped off a piece of chocolate. "I'm trying to remember if you've met my partners."

"No." *Of course she was in the platonic category*. "But Harry did. He said the bravest thing he'd ever done was say no to Jordan King about the hotel development."

There was a wealth of affection in Luke's laugh. "His bark's worse than his bite and it's Christian's charm you've got to watch. We're taking a softly-softly approach this time around."

"I'd guessed as much." Liz thought of the basket of toys, never used. "You must miss them."

"Hell, no. They've found soul mates and are pushing the happy-ever-after doctrine with the zeal of religious converts and the finesse of second-hand-car salesmen." He shuddered. "Thank God their women have more sense."

"You approve of their choices, then?" From the bitterness in his voice, she'd thought perhaps he didn't.

"Wholeheartedly. Except I made the mistake of saying once, 'I'll get married again if I can find women like yours.'" He shook his head.

She chuckled. "And now they're combing the kingdom."

"Hey, wait until your friends try to set you up. Then see how funny you find this."

Her stomach swooped. "My friends were also Harry's friends, they know not to try… Listen, I know I've just set up a game, but will you take a raincheck? I have to be up at six tomorrow."

"When did you last have a day off?" he asked abruptly.

"When did you?" she countered.

She thought she'd won but he rallied. "This Saturday at the wedding." He yanked her wet towel off the back of a chair and handed it to her. "You know, why *don't* you come with me? King events are always memorable."

"You're already taking Fred, remember?"

"Even better. As Fred you'll be completely anonymous. The wedding's being held at Kez and Christian's farm on the Hauraki Plains, so there are no paparazzi. And you said my friends don't know you by sight."

The temptation to get away from the fishbowl of preelection campaigning was beguiling. "They're bound to come to Beacon Bay sometime."

"So what? You'll be secure in another three-year tenure and the joke will be even funnier."

Liz wished she had his confidence in her future. Yesterday's campaign hiccup meant she'd have to work even harder to make up ground. And her batteries were already so flat, she needed jumper cables to get started in the morning.

"Well, Fred? You want to have some fun as Rent-A-Date?"

The clarification of her role removed Liz's last doubt. One day…it wasn't much to steal for herself. "You're on."

CHAPTER SEVEN

"Surname?"

Liz had no idea what Luke had chosen for Fred. "Flintstone?"

The security guard scrutinized her through mirrored sunglasses that reflected an anxious and disheveled blonde. "Hold still a minute." Liz pulled the loose strands of her hair into a tidier chignon and checked her appearance again. Under the sunglasses the guard suppressed a smile.

"Look for Fred...Luke Carter's date." Racing around country roads trying to find a stranger's wedding... Why the hell was she doing this?

He checked the list, grinned, then pressed the controls for the gate to open. "I was expecting a guy," he explained. "It was the exclamation marks the bride put next to your name."

Uh-oh. That didn't sound low profile to her. Liz

sped through, following signs to a paddock where
Mercedes, BMWs and Alfa Romeos baked in the sun
alongside 4WDs, station wagons and motorbikes.

Surrounded by a white picket fence on three
sides, the sprawling two-story Victorian-style
homestead bisected the green hill like a smile.
Grapevines wound around the trellis encircling the
bottom veranda. Below the house, the hill looked
as though it had burst its seams, spilling a mass of
colorful cottage-garden plants and flowers—blue
delphiniums, cabbage roses, lilac peonies and
orange nasturtium.

But Liz didn't have time to admire the view.
The bride and her entourage were about to leave
the house for the turreted marquee down to Liz's
right. She kicked off her high heels, picked them
up and ran, the Plains wind flattening her dress
against her body.

Grass green with a chiffon overlay, the skirt
flared from a fitted bodice with shoestring straps.
The dress had been an impulse buy last summer,
but it was too frivolous for mayoral functions and
she'd never worn it.

Outside the tent Liz slipped her shoes on and
scanned what seemed like hundreds of backs,
trying to find Luke's broad shoulders. Hopeless.

She was about to sneak into an empty chair at the back, when she saw him.

He stood at the front, wearing a suit that both civilized and accentuated his potent masculinity and exactly matched his eyes. As she tried to assimilate the fact that he was the best man, he saw her and smiled.

Beside him, the bridegroom stopped shifting from one foot to the other and glanced down the aisle. Dressed like Luke, and with his longish blond hair swept back, Jordan King looked dangerous.

Ice-blue eyes swept over her like a prison searchlight. Jordan said in a voice that could have carried Hannibal across the Alps, "Is that her?"

Two hundred people turned around. Involuntarily, Liz took a step back.

"We have a seat here for you, Fred." Jordan indicated the front row. "Come on up. To tell you the truth, I thought he'd made you up. Looks like I owe you a fifty, buddy."

Somehow Liz made it up the aisle, intensely conscious of everyone's interest.

Luke stepped forward, holding out a hand, and she grabbed it tight. He drew her closer and, realizing he was about to kiss her, Liz tried not to go rigid.

His warm lips brushed hers in a kiss so light

she barely felt it. Still, the sensation lingered as he shepherded her to a seat. "What happened?" he murmured.

"I got lost." Close up he looked hungover. "And you?"

"Don't ask." He sat her next to a beautiful brunette in an amber dress. "This is Kezia, Christian's wife. She'll look after you."

Liz had a fleeting impression of honey-brown eyes and a welcoming smile before the theme to *Rocky* emanated from her clutch bag. "Sorry…so sorry." She scrambled for her cell phone and switched it off just as the wedding march struck up, diverting everyone's attention.

Jordan lost his color.

"Want me to hold *your* hand now?" Liz heard Luke say sotto voce. Beside her, Kezia turned a laugh into a cough.

Jordan didn't answer; he was staring down the aisle with such tenderness that Liz forgave him for embarrassing her. Turning, she saw his expression mirrored in the face of a vibrant redhead wearing a garland of creamy flowers and a sexy wedding dress, and walking up the aisle on the arm of a silver-haired man.

The bride stopped dead. "Dad, we're in the

wrong place. My guy doesn't wear suits." With a grin, Jordan opened his jacket, revealing a coarse woolen waistcoat in a blue-and-black check pattern.

Everybody but Liz burst out laughing. Kezia whispered, "His Swanndri…priceless."

Huh?

Kate reached the front, mussed up the bridegroom's hair and surveyed the effect critically. "Much better." Liz was starting to feel like Alice in Wonderland. She looked at Luke, but, like everyone else he was grinning from ear to ear.

Jordan lifted his bride so they were breast to breast and kissed her so passionately she had to clutch her garland. "As usual, you're getting ahead of yourself," she complained, then cupped his face in both hands and kissed him back.

Tears pricked Liz's eyelids and she blinked them away. Kezia pressed a handkerchief into her hand.

Jordan set Kate on her feet. "But where are the bridesmaids?"

She grinned, suddenly appearing very like her bad-boy groom. "I couldn't have the matron of honor stealing my thunder, so I told them to wait."

Liz blinked, then glanced around to check reactions to this extraordinary admission. Everyone was smiling.

"Okay, girls," Jordan called. "You can come in now."

A roar of laughter started at the back, rolling forward row by row. Those near the front stood up, craning their necks.

At over six feet tall, the matron of honor was definitely a looker with beautiful blue eyes, incredible bone structure…Liz started to giggle… and a scowl as black as his hair. Her giggle turned into laughter as more of this extraordinary apparition came into view.

Leading the other bridesmaids, he strode up the aisle, looking neither right nor left, his delicate rose-pink dress swinging against hairy calves. Diamanté sparkled on dainty ballerina slippers. At least they would have been dainty on smaller feet.

As he came closer, Liz noticed subtle differences to his outfit. He carried a bigger posy of creamy rosebuds, wore a delicate chiffon sash in the same matching pink tied in an extravagant bow at the back, a necklace of pretty pearls, which nestled against the light smattering of hair above his sweetheart bodice.

The guests howled; the bridal party clutched their ribs. The matron of honor's glare grew murderous, which only made him funnier. Wiping away tears of laughter with Kezia's spare hankie, Liz was suddenly very, very glad she'd come. *"Why?"* she managed to say between spasms.

Kezia, who was leaning on her for support, tried to catch her breath. "He once said…the day Jord got married…would be the day he wore a bridesmaid dress. Stupid."

"Very stupid," Liz agreed. "Who is he?"

Kezia started laughing again. "My husband."

LUKE STOOD next to the bride's father, Cliff, feeling about the same age, as Jordan and Kate were pronounced man and wife. His friend looked like a newborn, all the cynicism ironed out.

He tried to recall if he'd been that happy when he'd married Amanda. Seemed like his entire focus had been on trying to remember the vows she'd written for them. Some crap about being like swans that mated for life.

Later, Luke had learned that while some animal and bird species lived in lifelong pairs, it didn't preclude infidelity. Oh, yes, he'd enjoyed the irony.

Jordan picked up Kate's hand and kissed the palm. Her fingers curled around his and Luke thought, these two good people will last. This is real.

Christian and Jordan had joined a club he couldn't belong to, and as much as Luke rejoiced in his friends' happiness, it only threw his own failure into sharp relief. The old ties were dissolving and he felt a profound loss.

Then the wedding march played over the sound system, the bride and groom led the way down the aisle and he turned to offer his arm to the matron of honor. "Ma'am?" Christian scowled. "C'mon, sweetie, stop playing hard to get."

Disgusted, Christian grabbed his arm. "You'll pay for this."

"Nothing to do with me, pal."

"Don't lie, Jordan hasn't got this much design flair."

Okay, maybe they'd had help with the feminine touches. Luke winked reassuringly at Kezia. "Yeah, well—" he shrugged, accepting the fall-guy role "—it was worth it."

Beside Kezia, he saw Liz, mascara streaked, her lashes clinging damply to her flushed cheeks, and he grinned. Her answering smile was wide and unguarded. Friends, Luke reminded himself. "See you outside, Fred."

Christian's gaze sharpened with interest. "That's Fred? She's—"

"Blond. Yeah, I know. And you owe me fifty bucks."

They stepped out into the full glare of the early-afternoon sun. Pain stabbed behind Luke's eyes and he dug in his pocket for his sunglasses.

"Still hungover from the stag?"

"Yeah."

"Good." Christian dropped his arm. "Now, if you'll excuse me, I'm going to change into man clothes."

Luke caught the chiffon bow at the back of his dress. "Oh, no, you don't. The wedding's not over yet. And you've got damn smug since you embraced moderation."

Christian twisted in his hold. "Even in the old days I would never have been dumb enough to challenge Jordan to a drinking game. Now, let go before I deck you."

"Hey, Jord!" Luke hollered.

Flicking his bow out of Luke's hand, Christian said with great dignity, "You, sir, are no gentleman."

The bridegroom looked over at the sea of well-wishers that had swallowed his bride, then strolled over. "The whole wedding, bud, that was the bet."

Christian picked up a flute of champagne from

the tray of a passing waiter and downed it. "You and Luke want this on your conscience? Huh?"

Jordan and Luke exchanged glances. "Okay," Jordan conceded. "You can lose the posy."

"Where's the gun?" Christian demanded. "I'm going to shoot myself."

"Locked away," said Jordan. "You think I'm stupid?"

Christian untied the bow and pulled off the sash. "Fine, I'll hang myself with this."

Kezia, who was approaching with Liz, said practically, "Honey, chiffon won't hold your weight."

Christian's eyes narrowed as he looked at his wife. "You know an awful lot about this outfit." In fact, she and the bride had spent many happy hours on it.

Kezia instinctively edged closer to Liz, which Luke found interesting. Despite her slender frame, the mayor had an innate authority that inspired confidence. Liz didn't let Kez down. "That's because I told her."

"Welcome, Fred." Christian shook her hand. "But how would you know?"

There was only the barest hesitation before she said, "I designed it."

"That's how Fred and I met." Luke went to stand beside her. "Why do you think your outfit has so much darling detail? I had to find excuses to keep going back."

Lightly he draped his free arm around her shoulder but Liz wasn't expecting it and jumped. Three pairs of eyes narrowed.

Valiantly, she tried to make up for the revealing gesture by slipping an arm around his waist, then looked around nervously for the waiter. "I think I'll join you in that drink, Christian."

"Nice try," he answered, "but I've worked out who the real culprit is." The twinkle in his eye became a glint as he turned to his wife. "You. To the house. With me. Now."

Kezia's lips twitched as she found Liz a flute of champagne and handed it over. "Why?"

"If I have to wear a damn dress, I want to do something masculine in it." He grabbed Kezia by the arm and started marching her to the house.

"Shouldn't we save her?" Liz asked anxiously. Then Kezia put her arm around the bridesmaid's manly waist. "Oh."

Something soft brushed against Kezia's bare legs and looking down, she saw a lamb heading toward the small groups now milling in the garden. "Um, is that animal supposed to be here?" Right now, anything seemed possible.

Jordan scooped up the lamb and called to two boys maneuvering a radio-controlled Batmobile around the guests. "Dil-boy, John Jason. You wanna take Dog back to the paddock?"

Liz shot Luke a sideways glance. "Of course the lamb's called Dog," she murmured.

Grinning, he squeezed her shoulder, his palm warm and callused on her bare skin. "Kez and Christian's toddler still gets confused."

"I know how she feels," said Liz.

He winked at her. "Told you you'd have fun, Fred."

"So how long have you two been dating?"

Liz had been ambushed in the bedroom-turned-cloakroom by a disparate group of women that included the bride, Kate; Megan, one of the groom's Amazonian sisters; and Bernice May, an extraordinary old lady whose penciled brows were as acute as the intelligent eyes underneath them.

"Two months," said Liz. They might not have come up with a surname but she and Luke *had* discussed this.

"Is it serious?" Megan asked the question casually enough but her hands tightened around the stem of her champagne glass.

Luke had instructed Liz to answer an emphatic yes to that question, but faced with Xena, Warrior Princess, Liz chickened out. Apparently Jordan's youngest sister had hero-worshipped Luke for years.

"You'll have to ask Luke."

"Well, I'm ticked." Bernice May untucked the champagne bottle from under her arm and refilled everyone's flutes with a liberal hand, ignoring Liz's demur. She herself was drinking beer. "Luke was going to be rebound guy now Jordan's off the market."

The bride looked down at her white satin Manolos, said meekly, "I'm sorry for stealing Jordan."

"Apology accepted." The old lady took a swig from her Steinlager and her pearls clunked against the base of the green bottle. "I was going off him anyway. Call me shallow but I can't feel the same about him since he cut his long hair."

Everyone looked expectantly at Liz who was finally getting the hang of how things worked around here.

"I guess you saw Luke first," she conceded reluctantly.

Mollified, Bernice May patted her hand. "Tell me he's useless in bed and I'll relinquish my claim."

"Not entirely useless." Liz sipped her champagne. "That washboard stomach is great for balancing a teacup."

She jumped as two warm hands tightened around her neck, then dropped to give her shoulders a gentle massage. "Fred's a great kidder," said Luke behind her. "She did a year at clown school but had to drop out." She felt him shrug. "Not funny enough. I think it was the chicken suit, pumpkin."

Liz leaned back against him. "But we found another use for it, didn't we, cabbage?"

His long fingers found a sore spot and dug deep. She tried not to wince.

"What *do* you do, Fred?" said Bernice May, tucking a gray curl behind her ear. One false crimson nail stayed behind.

Liz retrieved the nail and handed it back to her. "Manicurist."

Bernice May tucked the nail into her purse. "Don't suppose you carry a repair kit?"

"Sadly, no."

"I have one," said Kate, a sparkle in her hazel eyes. "Let me get it."

Liz tensed and Luke's fingers returned to the knotted muscles. "Won't do you any good," he said lazily. "Fred's a pet manicurist. Specializing in shih tzu."

Liz met Kate's eyes, read her amusement and had to bite her lip.

"There can't be much money in *that!*" Megan was jealously watching Luke's hands on Liz's shoulders. Liz was intensely conscious of them herself.

"Enough to fund her Irish dancing," he said.

Kate started to laugh, but Bernice May pricked up her ears. "Michael Flatley, now, *there's* a rebound guy."

That finished everyone off.

"Okay, you two," Kate said when they'd stopped laughing. "Keep your secrets—while you can."

"Fred, did I tell you about the time I first met Kate?" Luke reminisced. "It was at a surprise party for Jordan, only his friends and family got the biggest surprise. We caught them—"

Liz ducked as Kate threw a pillow at him. "Bring that up during the speeches and I'll kill you, Luke Carter, do you hear me?"

"No pillow fights until after the photos," he countered. "Which reminds me, we're needed in the garden."

"Don't worry about Fred." Bernice May refilled Liz's champagne glass. "I'll look after her."

CHAPTER EIGHT

SIPPING HER CHAMPAGNE, Liz sat on a garden bench with Bernice May listening to heat-drowsy bees, and watching Luke pose for photos with the bridal party amid the red roses.

Other guests smiled and nodded, sometimes stopping for a brief chat as they wandered between the house and the marquee, now being reconfigured for the reception.

Bernice May introduced Liz as the quirky Fred, a former clown turned dog manicurist, most notable for being the woman lucky enough to be sleeping with the drop-dead-gorgeous Luke Carter.

No one chewed her ear about rate rises or council policy. No one expected her to be intelligent, impartial and sensible. Liz pulled at her French twist and her fine hair fell around her shoulders.

Sun protection, she told herself, trying to

remember when she'd last worn her hair down. Years. Long before she'd met Harry.

Her sense of well-being was headier than the champagne bubbles, more piquant than the surrounding flowers.

Luke glanced over to make sure she was okay. Fluttering her fingers, she blew him a kiss and his eyes blazed a lazy warning.

Maybe she had a tiger by the tail, but Liz was having too much fun as Fred to let go. Since finding out about her past, Luke had stopped flirting with her, and behind her relief was a woman's pique that he could switch off his attraction so easily.

"He still hasn't forgiven you for that crack about how lousy he is in bed," noted Bernice May. "You're in for it, later."

"I'm driving myself home tonight, so I'm safe." Liz put the slight pang in her stomach down to hunger. It was now two o'clock and she hadn't eaten since breakfast. "Which also means no more champagne." The old lady was still carting around her bottle like a geriatric genie.

"You won't be driving for hours yet." Bernice May removed Liz's hand from the top of her glass and refilled it.

Politely sipping her champagne, Liz glanced back to the bridal party. "Wow," she said softly.

The photographer had positioned the three men for a buddy shot. The breeze ruffled Luke's dark hair and molded Jordan's thin silk shirt against his impressive frame. He'd already dispensed with the waistcoat and jacket. And no dress could detract from Christian's charismatic masculinity.

They all smiled for the camera, the shot was taken and the group broke up. Jordan rejoined his bride and sisters; Christian wandered over to Kezia and took their small daughter from her arms. Luke sought the shade of a magnolia and stood alone, his expression shuttered, his arms folded.

Instinctively, Liz stood. But Jordan's sister, Megan, peeled off from the others and approached him with two glasses of champagne. Feeling silly, Liz sat down again. Of course he wasn't lonely.

Bernice May waved to Jordan's mother, a tiny woman to have produced so many tall children. "Lemme go find out when the food's being served. We want pole position at the buffet."

Aware of being slightly tipsy, Liz put down her champagne glass. Was this her third? It was hard to tell when Bernice May kept it filled. As she tried to count back, a rodent was thrust under her nose. Seeing white rats was not a good sign.

"Wanna pat it?" asked a gleeful voice.

Turning around, Liz saw the six-year-old lamb-catcher she'd met earlier. A lick of light brown hair fell across his forehead and he looked a lot dirtier now. She adopted a stern expression. "You were hoping I'd scream, weren't you?"

"It works sometimes," he admitted cheerfully.

Behind him the older boy shuffled his feet. "I told him not to do it." Skinny, small-boned with expressive brown eyes and wearing clothes that looked too big for him, he was obviously feeling the moral weight of being the oldest.

"I bet it's funny when you do get screams though," Liz said, and the boys cracked grins. "I'm trying to remember your names.

"I'm Dillon," said the bigger boy, "and this is John Jason."

Liz scratched the rat behind the ears. "I always wanted a pet when I was a kid but I couldn't have one."

John Jason looked interested. "Have you got one now you're old?"

She blinked, then laughed. "No, my hus…the person I lived with was allergic. I've been thinking about getting one lately." Except the thought of being solely reliant on an animal for companionship depressed her. Suddenly Liz did feel old.

"Luke said you cut dogs' toenails," Dillon said and her mood lightened. That man would pay. Because the boys were obviously impressed, she invented a few stories that made their eyes widen, then told John Jason his rat had the best cuticles she'd ever seen.

"I didn't know rats had cuticles," Luke said. He'd taken off his jacket and tie and undone a couple of buttons on his shirt under the silver-gray waistcoat, which moved with his body like a second skin.

Dillon turned around eagerly. "Luke, did you remember to bring your medals?"

"Yeah, they're in the car." He threw the boy the keys. "Don't bite them this time, John Jason."

The boys raced off, whooping at the top of their lungs. Dillon stopped, yelling, "I like your girlfriend!"

Luke turned back to Liz. "So do I…when she's not slandering my reputation as a lover."

She refused to blush. "You can talk, cutting dogs' toenails, Irish dancing… I sound like a complete flake. Thank you, I haven't had so much fun in years."

"Good." He sat down and began rolling up his sleeves, revealing builder's forearms. He had a cut across one knuckle on his left hand. "You look gorgeous by the way." He said it casually, as though it was true, and this time she did color up.

"So do you." Realizing she was staring, Liz glanced down at the bridal party. "I gave the game away earlier, didn't I? Jumping when you touched me?"

"Blowing me a kiss was a nice counter. With a little work I think we can swing the balance in our favor."

He rested his arm along the bench behind her, and tipped his champagne glass to hers with a slow sexy smile that made her blink.

Distracted, Liz sipped her champagne, the fizz on her tongue matching the one in her blood. "Be careful with those molten glances," she warned. "Fred might be able to handle them but Elizabeth is prone to palpitations."

His laugh rang out across the garden.

"Hey, you two." Jordan strode up the hill. "We need you both down here for a group shot."

"No!" Liz reacted instinctively. "Besides, it wouldn't be right." She realized she wasn't playing her part and added hastily, "I mean, I take *terrible* pictures. Ruin every shot I'm in. Moonfaced." She looked to Luke for support.

"Oh, I don't know, pumpkin." He lifted her hand and kissed it, deliberately teasing her. "Those Polaroids I took of you on the sheepskin came out okay. Different moon of course." When she frowned at him he turned to Jordan and said easily, "We're staying under the radar as long as we can."

His friend looked at Liz. "Jealous ex?"

A shadow passed over her eyes, and Luke answered for her. "Something like that."

"We still need you, buddy."

"I'll be right down." He waited until Jordan was out of earshot. "Sorry."

"It's fine," she said in her mayor's voice.

He hesitated. "When I saw you accept a hankie from Kezia, I did wonder whether seeing all this happy-couple stuff was difficult for you. It wasn't something I considered when I asked you to come."

"Don't worry about it, I always cry at weddings. And frankly, my own isn't something I get nostalgic over. Harry insisted we do it loud and proud, but I had to cough wherever I went to save people the embarrassment of being caught talking about how long our marriage would last." She laughed. "My throat was raw by the end of the day."

She was expecting him to smile, so Luke did, but he thought it a pity that she'd had no family to take her side. Knowing her background explained so much about her, including why she'd been attracted to an older man. Security.

"How about yours?"

For a moment he forgot what they were talking about, then he grimaced. "Completely out of hand…turtledoves, pink champagne, balloons in the shape of hearts and Amanda so stressed she slapped my hand away whenever I touched her."

Her dark eyes danced. "Better luck next time."

"There won't be a next time."

"You sound sure."

He shrugged. "I don't have the gene for emotional intimacy. Amanda left me for someone who did."

Liz said nothing, simply brushed her knuckles against his cheek.

Abruptly, Luke caught her hand. "I don't accept pity, either."

"Actually I was trying to return the empathy you showed me the other night," she said mildly, and tapped their joined hands against his cheek, harder this time. "Much tougher to be the recipient, isn't it?"

Understanding passed between them, unexpected and surprising. Ruefully, he released her hand. "Much tougher…sorry."

Then because he needed to remind himself why kissing her wasn't a good idea, he gestured to John Jason and Dillon, who were tearing back across the field with his medals. "You're great with kids. I'm surprised you and Harry never had any."

"Luke!" Jordan shouted from the garden. Raising a hand in acknowledgment, he lingered, curious to hear Liz's reply.

She smoothed out her dress. "He didn't want more children."

"What about you?"

Liz clasped one wrist. "I made my decision when I married him."

He needed to know where she stood on relationships, so Luke pushed. "It's not too late, you're only thirty-five."

But she was shaking her head before he'd finished. "I won't get married again."

Before Luke could ask further questions, the boys arrived, panting like overheated puppies, and a shrill whistle recalled him to his duties.

"Later," he said, and it was a promise.

LUKE HADN'T EXPECTED to enjoy this wedding.

He'd already tried to resurrect the old Luke on the stag night, but alcohol had only exacerbated his sense of alienation. Whatever happened to the workaholic wunderkind, too damn busy being successful to think about nebulous bullshit like the meaning of life?

But tonight he was having fun. On the dance floor he sent Liz into a spin and admired her legs as the green dress swirled. Her arms, lightly tanned, gleamed under the lights.

He was finding it difficult to equate the collected, controlled mayor with the woman before him, all flying hair, flushed cheeks and smart mouth, and with a way of moving that in any other woman Luke would have considered foreplay.

For all her political astuteness, he'd sensed a sexual naïveté in Liz.

If she wasn't naive she wouldn't be teasing him with affectionate touches and flirtatious remarks. If she wasn't naive she wouldn't assume that because he was her friend she was safe.

Her expectation that he'd behave himself amused him as much as her mistaken belief that he was no longer attracted to her because he'd stopped flirting with her this week.

He hadn't backed off because he wasn't interested; he'd backed off because he was too interested. Elizabeth Light was a complex woman, and his life didn't need any more complications. But she'd removed the biggest hurdle earlier this afternoon when she'd told him remarriage wasn't on her agenda.

The dance ended, and Liz fell against him breathless and laughing—a warmhearted infectious sound that caused dancers nearby to smile.

He caught her against him, enjoying her exhilaration. "Fred, those Irish dancing lessons have really paid off. You're not standing on my feet anymore."

"Because you don't move them, they're easy to avoid. But I need a rest."

"You're supposed to be gazing into my eyes, Fred, not insulting me." Their table was deserted; everyone else was still dancing. Luke pulled out her chair and sat down beside her. "My friends are watching us," he lied, "so now would be a good time."

Liz lowered her chin, glanced up at him with wide eyes. "How's this?"

"Too Bambi."

She tilted her head, shot him a sideways glance through half-closed lashes. "This?"

"You look like you need a chiropractor."

"Fine," she said, exasperated, "I'll count the flecks in your irises." She leaned closer and concentrated. "One…two…" Liz had always thought them steel in color, but this close they were as ethereal as smoke. "Two…three."

"You said two already."

She started again. "One, two…"

His pupils dilated until they were black orbs ringed by silver. Unleashed, his expression was seductively predatory. Suddenly she was nervous. "I'll get us some water."

Luke said nothing as she stood, but as she walked past, Liz found herself hauled onto his lap.

She tensed under the hot reality of contact, planting her hands on his broad chest to steady herself. Under her one palm, his heartbeat was slow and regular. He lifted her hand and kissed the racing pulse point on her wrist. "Are we going to do anything about this?"

"No." She forced herself to relax, deeply conscious of the heat of his body scorching through her thin dress.

"Do you expect to be celibate for the rest of your life? If so, I think you're being unrealistic. We've been striking sparks off each other for weeks."

Her spine poker stiff, Liz sat on Luke's lap and

tried to match his objectivity. "I expect I'll have an affair…eventually. When I work how to tell a guy he's only temporary. I don't want to hurt anyone."

"I can do casual," he invited. "And you can't hurt me."

She focused on his chin. "You don't understand. I can never replace what I had with Harry."

"It's because I understand that that I'm making this offer. You're not looking for love because your marriage was perfect, I'm not looking for love because my marriage was a disaster."

"Even if I was tempted…" She found the courage to look at him and realized she'd been wrong in thinking Jordan King was the wild one. "I can't do anything to jeopardize my chances of reelection. Having a fling with you would be—"

"Crazy. You're right." Lightly he trailed a finger down her arm. "But tonight I'm here with Fred, not the mayor of Beacon Bay. And Fred could stay the night—if she chose to." He looked at the goose bumps he'd raised and smiled. "Think about it."

CHAPTER NINE

SHE DID.

Disgusted with herself, Liz did think about it.

Through the rest of the evening, through the bouquet toss, through the cutting of the cake, the last speeches and departure of the bride and groom in the helicopter, she tallied and retallied all the sensible reasons to say no.

And when she'd exhausted those, she invoked the illogical and very feminine ones. He hadn't even kissed her, they hadn't properly dated…the offer was totally irregular and strangely detached.

Which also made it exciting, freeing and outrageously tempting.

Late in the evening, she watched Luke slow dance with Bernice May. He moved with an athlete's grace, but with his waistcoat undone, his sleeves rolled up and his dark hair slightly disheveled he looked like a gambler. And tonight she was the prize.

All credit to him, he'd done nothing—verbally or physically—to persuade her since making his offer, giving her space to make a sensible and objective decision.

Liz sighed.

Over Bernice May's birdlike shoulder, Luke smiled at her, his teeth wolf white, and she escaped to the deck to think. Leaning over the balustrade, she stared blindly into the night.

She wanted Luke but her feelings were knotted and complicated. Harry might be inviolate in her heart, but that didn't mean she wouldn't feel guilty sleeping with someone else. And while Luke might be sexy, smart and honest, he was also cynical, bitter and disillusioned.

He'd said she couldn't hurt him, yet there was a dark loneliness underneath his easy confidence. She recognized it because she shared it. Liz sighed again.

"Penny for them."

Kezia's warm voice came from the shadows and she spun around. The other woman was leaning on the balustrade farther down the deck, half hidden by a grapevine. Deep in thought, Liz hadn't registered the faint rose perfume. Now she realized Kezia had been there all the time.

"I was admiring the view." To back up her claim, Liz looked skyward. The stars were so bright they looked like miniature suns scorching holes in the night. The bleached moon, just waning, cast silver beams on the undulating farmland. "You live in a magical place."

"It's a great place to think, too." As Kezia joined Liz, the band struck up the tango and a burst of hilarity drew their attention. Through the window they watched Bernice May—a rose between her teeth—tighten her grip on a protesting Luke.

Both women started to laugh.

"You might want to rescue your man," Kezia suggested.

Liz hesitated. Over the afternoon and evening the two of them had struck up a rapport—maybe because they were the only sane ones in this crazy menagerie. "He's not mine," she confessed as they turned back to the view. "We're faking it."

"I thought so at first," Kezia said gently, "now I'm not so sure."

"Oh, the friends part is real."

"Really?" Kezia gestured to two chairs and they sat down. "That makes you a lot more interesting than a girlfriend. Luke is very selective about his friends."

Her husband's roar of laughter emanated from inside and, eyes twinkling, she added, "*These* days, anyway. So why the sigh?"

Married to one of Luke's best friends, maybe Kezia could offer an insight that would help Liz's decision. "I am considering a temporary…upgrade in our friendship," she admitted a little awkwardly.

"And you're worried about jeopardizing your friendship?"

Liz knew this sensible woman would understand.

"Partly." An image of Luke standing apart from his friends this afternoon flashed into her mind. "Can I hurt him?"

Kezia stared at her intently. "You obviously think so, or you wouldn't be asking."

"He says I can't."

"Luke always says what he means and means what he says."

Kezia wasn't going to give Liz a straight answer, how could she? Luke was her friend.

"Well, thanks for your help."

Kezia obviously sensed her disappointment. "I'm not trying to be obtuse, but in a lot of ways Luke is an enigma. If you really want my advice—" she smiled "—trust Fred's instincts."

LIZ TOOK A DEEP BREATH. "I've made a decision."

"Let's hear it."

The band struck up a schmaltzy love song and she had to raise her voice. "I've decided to go home."

"Okay." She waited for more. "Sorry, I didn't realize you meant now," he added.

Luke stood up from their table and, stunned, Liz followed his lead. All that agonizing, she thought, and he doesn't care either way?

Bernice May was the one who protested. "Change your mind and drive home in the morning."

"It's a ninety-minute drive and she's got an early appointment," Luke said.

She did; still, Liz resisted an impulse to hit him.

The old lady made an impatient gesture. "So get up early. You young people have no stamina." To Liz's intense embarrassment, she pulled her aside and whispered loudly, "If it's noise you're worried about, he's got the guest cottage to himself."

Luke overheard. "Let it go, Bernie. She's made up her mind."

It would serve him right if she changed it. Finding it increasingly difficult to hold her smile, Liz said her farewells. Kezia hugged her; Christian kissed her on the cheek.

"It's been a pleasure, Fred."

She barely knew these people and they treated her like one of them. Even the bride and groom, swamped by friends and family, had made a point of seeking her out to say a personal goodbye.

Outside, the music faded into the vastness of the country night as they followed the ghostly blue glow of solar lights along the track to the paddock where only a dozen cars remained. She should thank Luke for inviting her, but Liz was suddenly too angry for pleasantries.

How dare he get her all steamed up before sorting out his feelings?

The open farm gate, whimsically entwined with red, green and gold fairy lights, twinkled a direction across the tussock grass. There was no sea breeze to cool the humidity, and the chiffon dress wilted against her body. Liz felt like a deflated party balloon.

He'd obviously regretted the offer as soon as he'd made it.

She tried to read his face, stepped into a rutted tire track and stumbled. Luke caught her by the elbow in an iron grip. "Careful."

No, this wasn't a man who vacillated.

He took her car keys and opened her car door.

The interior light flicked on, illuminated the navy leather…and Luke's jaw. He was smiling.

"Of course," she blurted. "You're using reverse psychology to try to change my mind."

"What?"

Oh, God, she was wrong. "Listen, I had a wonderful time. See you at the lesson on Monday." She grabbed his hand and pumped it. The key he was still holding jabbed into her palm.

"Wait a minute. This just got interesting." His hand tightened on the car key as she tried to take it. All the remote politeness had disappeared from his tone. "Did you *want* me to try to change your mind?"

"No!" Honesty compelled her to add, "But a little more disappointment would have been nice."

"That tempted, huh?"

Her temper flared again. "Can I have my keys, please?"

He leaned against her car. "I'm worried you might interpret that as giving in too easily."

Liz gritted her teeth. "Trust me, I won't."

"You're really pissed about this, aren't you? The thing is, Fred, ambivalent women tend to have regrets. Regrets are complications. Neither of us wants complications." He sounded as if he was reciting by rote. "You'll thank me in the morning."

"Don't patronize me. I'm older than you are." All the logical arguments in the world and she had to choose the illogical one. Suddenly Liz was tired. "Give me the keys, Luke."

He opened his palm. "I want you to stay. But you have to be sure, Liz."

She grabbed the keys, sank into the driver's seat and slammed the door, then rolled down the window. "Would it have been so hard to just kiss me?"

Starting the car, Liz switched the headlights to high beam. A cow lifted its head from the trough in the next paddock. Water dripping from its mouth, it stared back with big, reflective eyes.

Distracted, she graunched the gears. "Listen, forget that, it was a stupid thing to say." Liz struggled to be her reasonable self again. "See you Monday."

"Make the first move, Fred, and I promise I'll make all the rest."

The huskiness in his voice made her skin hot, her pulse jump and stretched her nerves to breaking point. Her dress rustled as she lifted her arms and twisted her hair into a bun. Wisps escaped the knot, but her hands were trembling so Liz left them. Releasing the handbrake, she stared straight ahead and whispered, "I can't."

"That's okay, too." He stepped back, swallowed by the dark.

Halfway to the gate, Liz braked and backed up. "I'm not staying," she said through the open window, "but Fred wants to kiss you. Once."

If he'd shown any amusement she would have accelerated, but he simply nodded.

Before she could change her mind, Liz got out of the car, grasped Luke's arms in a straitjacket hold, closed her eyes and plunged. Her lips collided with his jaw.

Hopeless. She was hopeless at this. Embarrassed, she released him. His fingers closed around her arms.

"Try again."

"Okay." She took a deep breath, then to Luke's surprise, stepped closer and wound her arms around his neck. Her breasts—soft and full—pressed against his chest, her slender legs bumped his thighs.

Distracted by the feel of her, this time Luke didn't see Liz coming. Her mouth connected unerringly with his. Automatically, his arms came up around her waist. He waited.

The moon appeared from behind a cloud, flooding them with light. Her eyelids fluttered open. This close he could see every emotion. Confusion, desire, indecision.

His conscience pricked him. Maybe he shouldn't have encouraged this but dammit, he was only human. Then her lips, blood-warm, moved tentatively against his mouth, and her tongue, moist and sweet, teased for entry. Heat scorched south along male neural pathways and unleashed the self-restraint he'd practiced for too many weeks.

Catching her face in his hands, he opened his mouth and let her in, hungry for the taste of her, hungry for the feel of her, just damn hungry. His arms closed around her and he backed her up against the car, imprinting her body with his.

Deliberately, he sparked a long, languorous, slow-burning fuse of a kiss that fired closer and closer to the point of no return. He could feel her body grow heavier, melding to every muscle and sinew of his until he knew he had her.

Luke lifted his head. "Well?"

"I'll stay," she gasped.

"Are you sure?"

The resolve in her eyes wavered. "Yes, but..." There was always a but. "I don't want to use you, Luke."

It was a crazy thing to say given his erection was pressing against her stomach and she was clutching his open waistcoat in a death grip, but despite his amusement, he felt a warmth that had nothing to do with anything physical. All his life people had used him—his athletic ability, his fame and his wealth.

Luke leaned forward. "I'm giving you permission," he whispered in her ear, and on a shiver she turned her head and captured his mouth. He put no brakes on this kiss—hot, deep and carnal—it was designed to bypass her last scruples. Instead, her surrender shattered his self-control.

Legs like jelly, Liz clutched Luke's shoulders, lost in the incredible sensations aroused by his tongue. He slid a hand up to cup one of her breasts, his thumb beside her nipple, and she ached for his touch but remorseless, he let his hand lie, burning her through the chiffon bodice.

Gasping, Liz shoved him away. "No teasing. I can't stand it."

"If I touch you," Luke said hoarsely, "I'll take you right here."

She dug her nails into his shoulder. "If you keep looking at me like that I'll let you."

"That does it." He grabbed her hand and hauled her back toward the house, swerving left down a garden path leading to the dark shape of the guest cottage.

Stumbling to keep up with him, Liz stepped out of her heels and left them behind. The gravel path was sharp under her tender feet; but she didn't care.

"One time only," she reminded him.

"One night only," he corrected. "It's going be more than once."

Liz felt dizzy. "And this won't affect our friendship."

"No, back to normal tomorrow."

She knew at this point they'd promise each other anything. Still, there was a reassurance in talking about tomorrow. Because right now was getting scary again.

As they reached the door, the security light came on, shining off Luke's dark hair, casting shadows across his face, grimly intent as he used his key. His gaze lifted to hers and his pupils were wide and fathomless.

She gulped.

"Too late," he said and pulled her inside.

CHAPTER TEN

THROUGH THE DOOR'S antique glass the security light painted the hallway in monochromatic shades of soft whites and sharp-edged black.

Liz held tighter to Luke's hand as he led her farther into the darkness. He squeezed her fingers. "Lights on or off?"

She swallowed. "On." Reluctant as she was to be seen naked, she couldn't be ashamed of this.

There was a click, and the room was suffused in a golden glow. The homestead was a clever combination of classic and modern but the guest cottage made no compromises. Light gleamed off the polished kauri floorboards and ceiling, struck the brass candlesticks on the tiny ornamental fireplace.

The walls were an eggshell blue, the curtains extravagant billows of dusky pink. Luke's clothes were strewn over a tiny pedestal table and equally dainty chairs but it was the bed that caught Liz's attention, with its headboard of finely wrought Victorian brass, delicate crocheted white bed-spread and feather pillows.

Pristine. White. Waiting.

Her heart started to pound harder. Luke pulled the drapes over the bay window, shutting out the world, and turned around. The room's delicate femininity made him somehow more male, more dangerous and more potent. Maybe she'd tie him to that headboard and run.

She was conscious of her dishevelment, the dress clinging to her body in the hot night, the impropriety of sleeping with a man she didn't love.

He turned on an overhead fan and the soft whir stirred her blood. "Come over here," he said softly and the look in his eyes thrilled her with pleasurable terror.

"I'll meet you halfway."

"Whatever you say." She didn't understand his grin until he sprawled on the bed. As Liz bit her lip, he caught her in his arms and pulled her on top of him. "Relax, I won't bite—unless you want me to."

Liz pushed up until she was sitting astride him, hands planted on his chest, her green chiffon almost gaudy against the white sheets. She'd been about to remonstrate, but his words, the way he said them, and the feel of him, hard and hot between her legs, stopped her.

"Ah," he said, "you do want me to."

"I don't know what I want." But that wasn't true. She wanted sensual oblivion, to fill up all the empty, cold places with his heat, his vitality. For a little while.

He was watching her carefully. "You want to be touched," he said, wound her hair around his big hands and drew Liz down into a kiss that thawed her all the way through. His strong fingers brushed lightly over her face, her bare shoulders and arms, sensitizing and attuning her flesh to his. Stroking her everywhere except where Liz grew desperate to be stroked. Until she'd had enough of waiting.

Hands trembling, she wrestled with the buttons of his shirt, yanking it apart and running her hands down the smooth, warm pecs, his nipples, the ridges of his stomach, sliding her fingers along what she could reach of his incredible biceps. She'd wanted to do this for so long. She bent to lick a nipple, a flat disc against the muscle, and Luke groaned and stopped playing.

He shoved down her spaghetti straps, struggled with the zip at the back of her dress. She helped him, and the chiffon and satin fell with a slither around her waist. And then his hands were skimming over her breasts, thumbing her nipples at last. At last. Driving her crazy until she thrust them in his face because she had to have more.

His mouth closed on a nipple, he suckled, then moved to the other, circling, tugging, tormenting. On a gasp, she anchored her hands in his hair, soft under her restless fingers, and instinctively moved her lower body along his erection.

His large hands slid under her dress and cupped her bottom, encouraging the movement, and sensation started building too fast in her. Making love with Harry had always been tender and slow, a gentle buildup to a civilized release. But there was nothing civilized about this.

Liz released Luke's hair. "Stop!" But his mouth still hot on her breast, he tightened his hold, sliding her remorselessly over the edge. Her orgasm was convulsive, intense. She cried out and fell forward until his face was pressed between her breasts while her heart slammed against his cheek.

She was probably suffocating him but Liz couldn't move, the fan drying her light perspiration of heat and exertion and arousal. His husky laugh vibrated through her ribs and she forced herself to roll off him onto her back. Turning her head, she saw the male complacency in his expression and felt momentarily irritated. He looked so damn together. Then she smiled and kissed the tip of his nose. "Thank you."

Surprise flickered in his eyes. "I'm never going to work you out, am I?"

Not if she could help it. "Take off your clothes."

Luke grinned. As he got out of bed to disrobe, she squirmed out of the rest of her dress and burrowed under the sheet, cool and crisp against her overheated skin, then pulled off her panties.

The muscles in his back rippled as Luke shrugged off his shirt and turned around. Seeing her under the sheet, he smiled, but he said nothing as he unzipped his suit pants and let them fall.

Feet planted slightly apart, he let her look her fill before hooking his thumbs in his boxers, pulling her gaze down to the cut muscle of his abdomen where the V between his narrow hips was a visual arrow to his groin. And stepped out of them. Her throat tightened. There were some things she hadn't seen during their swimming lessons.

He gestured to the sheet. "Now you." Reluctantly, she dropped it to her waist. "Uh-uh. All the way, Fred. I like to look, too."

She kicked her feet free and concentrated on counting her toes.

The mattress sunk as Luke sat on the bed. "Do you know how long I've been imagining your body naked? I feel like a kid at Christmas, not sure what to play with first."

She smiled and pushed him back on the pillows. "Flatterer."

"I don't lie and in case you haven't noticed, neither does my body."

"I noticed." She'd admired his body from a distance for so long, it seemed incredible that tonight it was hers to explore. With her fingers, she traced the strong curve of his jaw, his lashes, sooty and thick, and the straight outline of his mouth. She pressed her lips to the pulse in his neck, drawn by the life there, nipped lightly.

He growled and reached for her, but she caught his hands and curled them around the brass bed head. "It's your turn."

His skin was surprisingly smooth over his un-dulating muscle. With her mouth and tongue Liz explored the dips and hollows and ridges of the compact muscle, shaking with increasing passion. There was a heady freedom in her emotional distance, safety in their friendship.

His knuckles were white on the polished brass long before she reached his narrow hips, the smattering of light hair below his navel.

Unceremoniously, she was hauled up his body, skin gliding against skin. "It's been too long for that." His voice shook, and Liz was glad because she didn't want this ferocity of need to be one-sided.

The rasp of his unshaven jaw brushed her cheek, sending a visceral shiver down her spine, then his mouth brushed hers.

Luke wreathed his fingers through her hair—champagne under the lamplight—and lightly pulled, exposing her throat to his kisses. She moaned. "There, yes, there."

Her responsiveness was driving him wild. Even in the throes of lust that had propelled him into an early marriage, he'd never experienced this primal urge to possess a woman.

Sex, he reassured himself, reveling in the feel of her skin against his, her vanilla-musk scent, her taste. It's just sex.

In passion, she was sloe-eyed, her irises indistinguishable from the pupils. Liz moaned again and Luke stopped caring what it was. He was in thrall to her body—silky skin, way too soft for a thick-skinned politician, curvy hips made to hold and touch-sensitive breasts. Moving his hand lower, he teased her until she was writhing.

"Get a condom, Luke. I can't take any more."

He tried to enter her slowly, conscious of how long it had been for her, but she wrapped her legs around him with a need that made him lose his self-control and he drove deep, almost savagely.

"Yes," she sobbed. "Like that."

Sex had always been a competitive sport to Luke, except the goal was to come in second. He was never so caught up in his own pleasure that he didn't satisfy his partner first, but Liz wouldn't let him be gentle or slow.

For the first time in his life he let a woman inflame him past caring into scorching release. In the aftermath, their torsos, slick with sweat, rose and fell against each other as they gasped for air.

They rolled apart, onto their backs, and let the overhead fan dry their sweat. When his breathing returned to normal, Luke turned his head and looked sheepishly at Liz. "I have no idea if you came or not."

Still in profile, her lips curved into a smile. "If I say no, can we do it again?"

Weakly he started to laugh and hauled her back into his arms. She was as boneless as a rag doll.

For long moments they lay in contented silence, her head on his chest. "Your heart *can* beat as fast as a normal person's," she said smugly.

"Lady, you'd kill a normal person."

As soon as he'd said it, Harry was an unspoken presence in the room. Shit. Cursing his big mouth, Luke stroked her hair, wondering if he would make things better or worse by saying more. As he agonized about it, something hot and wet trickled down his chest. Tears.

"Liz, I'm sorry."

"It's not what you think." She dried her eyes on a corner of the sheet. "I thought I'd feel guilty afterward. I don't. I'm so relieved."

He relaxed, realizing he hadn't hurt her. But then he couldn't let the moment pass—couldn't resist teasing her. Pulling away, he threw some uncertainty into his voice. "Are you saying it was… just sex?"

She sat up to look at him, the crazy woman, worrying about hurting his feelings. Kezia had mentioned Liz's concern. "Luke, I—"

He grinned. "Gotcha."

At 5:00 A.M. Luke was making her bacon and eggs. They were both starving. He sent Liz out to the vegetable garden for parsley and she paused to watch the fields expand into view under the rising sun, pulling his jacket closer around her bare shoulders. The dawn sky was the color of Luke's eyes…a soft, fresh gray.

He cooked in old jeans, low around his lean hips, and nothing else, and she couldn't resist leaning against all that solid muscle as she told him how she liked her eggs. Over easy. He turned them with a spatula; with his free hand he hauled her close.

She kissed his bare shoulder, warm and still damp from his shower. The pan forgotten, Luke nuzzled her neck, lifting her hair to reach the shiver spot he'd discovered last night. It scared Liz how quickly he'd learned her sensual secrets. They ended up eating their eggs hard and didn't care.

"Everyone will be up soon." She swallowed the last of her coffee. "I have to go."

Nodding, Luke rose from the breakfast table. She liked the way he respected her need for privacy. He'd also been careful to retrieve her shoes before they'd gone to sleep.

To Liz's relief, there'd been no dreams. Maybe, she thought as they walked across the dew-laden grass to her car, because Luke had kept waking her up to make love. Still expecting guilt or regret, she probed her feelings. Nothing. Their friendship had stopped the experience from being sordid. She linked arms with him, enjoying their physical closeness while she could.

At the car he lifted her hand and kissed it in a strangely old-fashioned gesture. "Will I see you again, Fred?"

For a moment, the happiness in his expression made her want to be reckless. But that would be foolhardy and she was a sensible woman. Still, her hand tightened instinctively on his. "No."

"Hell," he said lightly. "You accepted the offer to accompany that pampered shih tzu on a six-month cruise around the Med, didn't you?"

Releasing his hand, Liz dumped her bag in the trunk and turned on her cell phone. Ten messages. "What can I say? FrouFrou won't let anyone else touch her cuticles. We sail at eight tomorrow night."

"About the time I take my next swimming lesson with the mayor."

She hesitated. "Don't mention me, will you? I have a feeling she'd disapprove."

His eyes weren't dawn gray anymore, they were as reflective as a mirror. "If that's what you want."

"Don't you?"

"You have more to lose than I do." For some reason an image of him standing alone in the garden yesterday flickered into her mind, then his lips brushed hers in a farewell kiss that was almost impersonal. She didn't like it. Catching his shirt collar she kept him close, deepening the kiss until they were both lost in it.

While she still could, Liz released him. "So you don't forget Fred," she said unsteadily and got into her car. It smelled of reports and seat leather and responsibility. She forced herself not to glance in the rearview mirror as she drove away.

WHEN SHE WAS DRIVING on familiar roads again, Liz checked her messages.

The first was from a security contractor reporting vandalism to council buildings on Friday night. "Must have happened after our last check at 6:00 a.m., Mayor Light," said Bruce's slow voice. "Cleaners found it at ten, when they were emptying the wheelie bins. The whole back wall is covered in obscenities. A couple of houses nearby have been tagged as well. I need your okay to authorize the cleanup."

Liz listened for the time of call. 11.30 a.m. Saturday morning. Bruce had phoned again at noon and one, ending with: "I'll try and get hold of Deputy Mayor Patterson."

Jo Swann at the *Chronicle* left her first message late afternoon: "Heard about the graffiti. We're running a story and I'd like to talk to you." Her voice grew increasingly impatient over a further two calls. "We're going to press, and I really need an official comment." And finally, "No need to call back. Snowy's supplied quotes…. You know, Liz, your husband always made himself available."

And in between those, she listened to messages from Kirsty, initially breezy, progressing to irritated. "As your campaign manager, I should be able to tell people where the hell you are." But it was her last message that made Liz pull into a lay-by and punch in her stepdaughter's number.

"It's midnight and I'm really starting to get worried. I even got Nev to check your house in case…" Kirsty's voice trailed off. "I know I'm probably being paranoid but please, *please* phone when you hear this message and let me know you're okay. It doesn't matter what time."

Kirsty answered on the first ring.

"It's Liz and I'm fine. I just got your messages."

She heard a shaky indrawn breath. "Thank God!"

"I didn't mean to scare you."

Kirsty started to cry, and all the guilt Liz thought she'd sidestepped came crashing down on her head. Driving home late from a mayoral conference in Auckland, Harry had fallen asleep at the wheel and careened off the road, into dense scrub. His body hadn't been found for two days.

"All night," Kirsty sobbed, "I lie awake imagining your car crashed in a ditch somewhere. It's not like you to disappear without telling anyone… We were going to the police this morning."

"Oh, God…I'm so, *so* sorry."

Kirsty blew her nose. "So you should be. Where the hell have you been?"

"I…I…" *I've been enjoying wild sex with Luke Carter while you've been reliving the trauma of Harry's death.* "Staying at an old friend's out of town."

"*And* Jo Swann's been trying to get hold of you."

Liz seized the change of subject. "I hear Snowy covered for me."

"Oh, yeah." Kirsty gave a last sniff. "Once again the hero of the hour. Let me read it to you."

Liz heard the rustle of a newspaper. "'Council recently approved security cameras. Unfortunately there's a lengthy delay between approval and implementation….' Here's the good bit…. 'Let's just say one of my campaign policies is speeding up all this ponderous bureaucracy. I give my personal assurance to the community that security cameras will be in place this week—if I have to install them myself.' Hell," Kirsty finished glumly. "I'd vote for him."

Liz glanced at her watch. "I'm about forty minutes away. I'll come straight there to talk damage control.... And Kirsty? It won't ever happen again."

"It had better not."

Liz broke the connection and dialed Snowy's number. When he picked up, she let loose. "Aside from the fact that you know damn well security cameras are already scheduled for installation this week, you've no right to use your official role as DM for electioneering."

She took a breath. "'Ponderous bureaucracy' my ass. The only reason cameras were delayed was because your cronies kept raising spurious objections about cost."

"And here I was expecting a call of thanks for covering—to quote you—your ass," he said mildly. When Liz tried to answer, he talked over her. "And at least I was available in my official role."

He waited for comment but, suffering a resurgence of guilt, she had nothing to counter with.

"Liz," he cajoled, sounding like her old mentor. "This close to election, personality is bound to leak through, but I can assure you, any self-promotion was unintentional. So how about giving me the benefit of the doubt? I told Jo Swann that only something truly urgent would keep you away from your civic duties."

She closed her eyes. "I'm sorry. I overreacted. Thanks for covering for me."

By the time she'd rung and apologized to a chilly Jo Swann, Liz was close to hating herself.

And she definitely hated Fred.

CHAPTER ELEVEN

LUKE REALIZED he'd seriously miscalculated his comfort zone when the bus doors opened and the noise hit him like a sonic boom. And then fifty kids aged seven to fourteen thundered down the stairs and surrounded him, jostling, touching and yelling questions.

"Where do I sleep?"

"Is there a pool?"

"Someone said we have to eat spinach. Do we?"

Glancing around, he saw his staff was equally besieged. Except they were happy about it. "You'll be allocated camp counselors who'll answer all your questions."

Seeing their disappointment, he relented and said, "But you'll be sleeping in dorms, we swim at the beach so no pool and, yeah, there'll be some healthy food. But no spinach." With a straight face he added, "Brussels sprouts."

There was a universal groan.

"Hey, it was a joke." They looked at him dubiously.

"Mister. Mister. Mister!" He glanced down at the young girl tugging on his Camp Chance T-shirt. She had bossy written all over her pointed little face. "If I hate it, Mum says I can go home."

Luke disentangled himself and checked her name tag. "Hey, Moana, what kind of attitude is that to arrive with? You're going to love it here." He tried to sound encouraging but, sharp as a tack, she picked up on his irritation.

Immediately, she turned her back and, dark plait bobbing down her scrawny back, shoved her way through to Rosie. "Hey, lady. Lady! My mum says…"

Recognizing he was out of his depth, Luke rallied his staff, gave his welcoming speech, then like all good generals, left the front line ASAP. His contact with kids was limited to his partners' various connections and, with the exception of his goddaughter, tended to be superficial. Hand over his medals and his money and they generally left him alone.

Walking inside, he pulled his cell phone out of his pocket and scanned his messages, pausing as he saw one from Liz confirming their lesson tomorrow.

Last night he'd barely slept, restlessly alive to her heat, her scent, the rhythm of her breathing as she nestled against him in sleep. The whole purpose of having sex with the mayor had been to demystify this longing, unmask it for what it was—lust. Instead he felt edgy, vaguely dissatisfied, at odds with himself. He wanted more and he couldn't have it.

"Luke!" Rosie caught up with him. "You'll be joining us in the cafeteria for lunch, won't you?"

"I have a heap of work to do."

She looked shocked. "You *have* to share their first meal."

"Fine, I'll be there."

In his office, he shut the door and the kids' excited cries dropped to a background murmur. His staff was going to have to learn to do without him. A motivational talk tonight, a token visit every day, and he was done.

The council had approved the project—there might be a few tweaks after these kids had tested the facilities—but in the short term he could ease back until they'd gone.

Picking up the *Chronicle*, Luke planted his feet on his desk and settled back in his chair. Ten minutes later, his feet hit the floor with a thump. "Shit!" He stared at the paper in disbelief.

Commenting on the weekend's graffiti rampage, Beacon Bay Resident and Rate-payers president, Delores Jackson, raised an interesting question: "If we can't control our own hooligans, what on earth are we doing importing delinquents from Auckland?"

Following her quote, was a brief history of Camp Chance's development, including every conflict from the ethics debacle with Jordan last year to Delores's failed petition to have the camp relocated "away from civilization."

Swann's editorial made even more depressing reading. After doing a spot poll on the high street, she'd concluded that approval of the camp was only skin deep.

Scratch the surface and all the reservations are still there. Looks like Luke Carter still has his work cut out for him.

While he was glaring at the paper, the phone rang. "Carter."

"It's Caroline."

He made an effort to be pleasant. "Since when do planning consultants work Sundays?"

But she wasn't in the mood for small talk, either. "Listen, I've been studying the proposed new district plan and conditions are getting even more onerous. Remember your idea to make the camp less reliant on sponsorship? Save yourself more grief and submit an application for Resource Consent now."

With his free hand, he massaged the back of his neck. "Please tell me you're joking."

"Sorry, but I'm serious. Let me e-mail through what I have. Take a look at it and let me know."

He did take a look, then with a groan that came from the soles of his feet, set up an emergency three-way conference call with Christian and Jordan.

"Go for it," said Christian. "The sooner the camp's self-funding the better."

"Hell, we're only asking for another dorm and a variation on the camp's usage," said Jordan. "It's gotta be easier this time around." In the background Luke could hear a ukulele strumming a South Seas love song to the honeymooners. "Didn't most of council show up to the work bee?"

"Only because Liz persuaded them it would look good for the elections. Mayor Light," he added for clarification.

"We know who she is," Christian said.

Jordan distracted Luke from a sudden suspicion. "Surely the mayor's support counts for something?"

"If she's reelected." What would Liz do if she wasn't? He had a vivid image of her in a scarlet bikini under a Pacific Island sunset. "Jord, can you tell those crooners to knock it off? I'm finding it hard to concentrate."

The music stopped. "There's another option for you two," Luke said gruffly. "The camp was my idea, and there's no guarantee that we won't be throwing good money after bad. No hard feelings if you want to bail."

"So how is Fred?" Jordan asked.

Luke frowned. "Did you hear what I said? I'm committed but I completely understand if you—"

"She stayed over the night of the wedding," Christian interrupted.

"How the hell do you know that? We were so careful." Luke realized he was being deliberately sidetracked and his throat closed up.

"Kezia saw two pairs of footprints in the grass," Christian continued as though he hadn't spoken. "So are you two serious?"

"No," said Luke. "She doesn't like my pushy

friends." It was tough to keep the emotion out of his voice, but he managed it.

There was a muffled conversation between Jordan and his bride. "Kate thinks it's serious," he said when he came back on the line. "And her instincts are pretty good."

Luke knew it was useless to argue—about anything. "Okay, we're agreed. I'll submit a new application."

"Yep, we have a consensus, all right," Christian said. "We all think you should keep the mayor."

LIZ INTENDED to be coolly self-possessed when she saw Luke for their swimming lesson at 6:00 a.m. Bumping into him in the council foyer at three, however, threw her into a tizzy. "What are you doing here?"

Too late she heard the accusation in her tone. Her colleagues looked at her in surprise, and she pasted a smile on her face. Thank God she rarely blushed.

"Dropping off an application," Luke said easily, a gleam in his eyes. "You don't get rid of me that easy."

Liz felt a scorching rush of heat flush her whole body.

"Councillor Maxwell—" casually Luke turned

to the older man "—I hear you shot a hole in one last week?"

Beaming, Maxwell launched into a stroke-by-stroke account, which immediately halved the group, and Liz had privacy to pull herself together.

Luke interrupted Maxwell. "Much as I'd love to hear more about the course conditions that day, I should be getting back to camp." His expression was wry. "We're a supervisor short for kayaking and I've been volunteered. Mayor Light?" His tone was courteous but the amusement was still there. "Can I have a minute of your time outside?"

"I'm due in a meeting."

"It won't take long."

Convinced that everybody was staring, Liz followed him out.

"Relax, no one cares," Luke murmured as he opened the door for her.

Glancing back, she saw that he was right. Only Maxwell and Bray remained, still talking golf scores.

They faced each other on the broad steps. "If you react like this every time you see me in public, you'll blurt out a full confession before a week's up."

"Can you tell I was always the kid who got caught?"

"Except we didn't do anything wrong." He smiled uncertainly. "Did we?"

Liz's guilt centered on hurting Kirsty and neglecting her duties. But Luke himself? "No regrets," she said softly. Except perhaps that they wouldn't be doing it again. She looked away. "I need to get back."

There was a short pause. "I might be a little late tonight," Luke said. "I've been roped into staying for dinner again at camp."

Of course. The kids had arrived yesterday. Caught up in her own troubles, she'd forgotten. "How's it going?" Muscles rippled in Luke's biceps as he raked a hand through his hair, and she squashed an impulse to touch him.

"I'm getting sucked into the vortex." He grimaced. "And if you think dealing with Snowy's hard, you should meet Moana. I could do with your advice on handling bossy girls."

"You handled me okay." Her voice was too husky. What the hell was wrong with her?

Luke's eyes darkened. "Are you flirting with me, Mayor Light?"

She shook her head. "That would be foolhardy…under the circumstances."

"Yes, it would. I can probably keep my hands off you if you're resolved, but if you're ambivalent…"

"I'm not." She lifted her chin, hoping it would straighten her backbone, and looked at him. Immediately heat flared between them, the memory of their intimacy. Their need.

Luke smiled. "That's settled then."

Weakly she tried to protest. "Luke, I—"

"If you don't want me to seduce you tonight, Liz, don't come."

"That's not fair. You know there's only a week left until the mayoral swim."

He shrugged. "You should have thought of that before you started dithering—"

Now her backbone chose to straighten. "I don't dither!"

"I guess it's an age thing."

As she gasped in outrage, Snowy came around the corner of the council building. With difficulty, Liz schooled her expression. "You know from experience, Luke, that the submission process takes twenty-one days."

He folded his arms, the very picture of a disgruntled ratepayer. "At which point council asks for more information and they're off the hook for *another* twenty-one days."

"Ridiculous, isn't it?" Snowy said as he drew abreast, pressing an election pamphlet into Luke's hand. "And I promise that when I'm mayor there'll be a review of procedure."

"Which will drag on for two years," said Liz tartly, "cost thousands and tell us what we already know—we're underresourced."

Kindly, Snowy patted her shoulder. "You give up if you want to, Liz." With a wink at Luke he continued up the stairs.

Liz turned on Luke. "Don't you dare smile."

"You have to admire his gall. What are you countering with?"

She allowed herself a smidgen of smugness. "My 'invest in the community' initiatives will blow his out of the water."

"I don't know…" Luke scanned the pamphlet "His sound pretty good. A new community center and hall with an on-site crèche."

Liz snatched the pamphlet out of his hand and read it in disbelief before crumbling it into a ball. "That bastard."

"I can't believe I once thought you were repressed," Luke commented. "Go get him, killer."

She stormed into Snowy's office and threw the crumpled flyer on the desk. "You stole my ideas."

He looked at her, amused, over steepled fingers. "You don't have a patent on caring, Liz. Of course I have a social policy."

Smoothing out the paper, Liz read aloud. "'Improved channels of communication between community-group representatives and council…' It's almost word for word."

"Now, how could I know that?" he said reasonably. "Your manifesto hasn't been released yet."

It was supposed to be distributed through a letter-box drop tonight. Except now it would sound as if she was parroting Snowy.

Liz slammed her palms on his desk. "You promised me a clean campaign!"

"Imitation is the sincerest form of flattery."

"Snowy, you don't give a damn about pensioners and young families."

"I'll be a pensioner myself in three years. I was twenty when I started a family and now I have grandchildren to keep me in touch with young people's concerns. As I keep telling you, Liz," he reminded her gently, "there's no substitute for personal experience."

"Which is why," she countered, "I can name every community group that uses the center. I can tell you what their current issues are, I can tell you who their key volunteers are. I can even tell you which drawer in the kitchen they keep their clean bloody tea towels. You don't know that, do you?"

"No," he admitted, "but I will before the public meeting. And on the subject of kitchens, if you can't stand the heat…"

Not trusting herself to speak, Liz left his office and rang Kirsty. "Pull the pamphlet, we'll have to rework it tonight." She told her what Snowy had done, enjoying Kirsty's colorful annihilation of Snowy's character.

"Thanks, I needed that. So I'll see you after Harriet's gone to bed?"

"Sure. Listen, how about we rattle Snowy's cage with some door-to-door canvasing in his immediate neighborhood?" Kirsty suggested.

"Good idea."

Liz texted a message to Luke, asking if they could reschedule the lesson for the following morning, grateful for the reprieve. Almost immediately, her cell beeped an incoming message.

Cn do 6am. Xx Lke.

He'd never included kisses before.

For a split second she considered sending some back.

Liz sat down and put her head in her hands. She'd always been proud of her willpower, easily saying no to another piece of cake or a third glass of wine—secretly pitying those who were subject to their passions.

Now she knew what real temptation was. And the six-foot-three devil with the hell bod and heavenly smile had made it clear he wouldn't be kneeling alongside her while she prayed for self-restraint.

Opening her diary, Liz counted the days left until the swim challenge. Six. And this would be the second consecutive day she hadn't been in a pool. She'd advanced to synchronizing her arm movements and breathing, but she still couldn't sustain a crawl more than fifty meters. And she needed twice that by next week.

Retreat wasn't an option.

Setting the alarm on her watch, Liz gave herself permission to panic for five minutes. After Harry died, she'd used the technique to drag herself out of self-pity and the habit had stuck. The alarm beeped. Steeling her jaw, she got back to work.

Tomorrow she'd figure what to do about Luke. Today there were other fires to put out.

LUKE HAD EVERY intention of seducing Liz but, when he opened his front door the next morning, he saw at a glance that it wouldn't be today.

"How much sleep did you get last night?"

"Four hours."

Her hair was untidy—unusual for Liz—and the jacket of her summer weight tracksuit was unzipped, revealing the lime swimsuit underneath. A hanger of work clothes trailed off one shoulder and she carried her sports bag as though it held bricks.

He took it. "Tell me you ate last night."

Yawning, she stumbled into the house. "Kirsty ordered pizza."

Like that meant anything. Closing the door behind her, he followed her to the pool. "What about this morning?"

"Can't swim on a full stomach." She fumbled gracelessly out of her clothes, shivering in the slight chill of morning. "Let's do this."

"To hell with the swimming lesson." Picking up a towel, Luke wrapped it firmly around her shoulders. "I'm feeding you, then you're phoning in sick and going to bed. To sleep," he clarified when he felt her shoulders stiffen.

They slumped again. "Can't. Time's running out. Too much to do."

He resisted the urge to shake her. "You can't even form a coherent sentence, woman."

"Here's one. I'd rather be a ditherer than a nagger." Shrugging off the towel she jumped into the pool, making sure she splashed him.

Flicking water out of his eyes, Luke smiled.

"Fine," he growled when she surfaced. "We'll do the lesson. But you're not leaving before you've eaten breakfast."

He dragged off his wet T-shirt but stayed out of the pool. It was the only way he could keep his hands off her. Neither of them had time for an affair. It didn't matter. He'd seen the chink of indecision; that was enough for now. Management strategies could come later.

She mistimed her stroke and stood up, breasts rising and falling as she caught her breath. Her frustration was almost palpable.

"Come over to the side," he said.

He turned her around and, sitting with his feet dangling in the water, massaged her tight shoulders.

"I'm worried that I'm not going to make it," she admitted.

"Learning to swim is like learning to drive. Easy to learn the skills in isolation, but it's putting them together that's hard." His fingers teased out the knots. "Believe it or not, you're close to a break-through. All you have to do is keep practicing until it becomes automatic."

Liz leaned into those clever fingers, feeling the tension in her shoulders slowly ease. Almost as seductive as Luke's touch was his support. She closed her eyes and through the bliss of being stroked, felt her irritation flare. In one night this man had recolored her world with passion, laughter and excitement. Now she craved this from him.

"Relax." His warm breath on the back of her neck sent another shiver of sensory pleasure through her body. "I promise you'll be ready in time."

"Telling me what I want to hear," she said lightly. "That's a great seduction technique."

His fingers stilled on her wet shoulders. "I'll get breakfast."

Liz placed her hands over his. "That came out wrong. I'm not suggesting you'd lie to get me into bed." She leaned her head back against his chest to look up at him, aware that she was making herself vulnerable. "I'm using humor to try to minimize how your touch makes me feel, something else I obviously need to practice."

Luke tightened his hold. "And how do I make you feel?"

For too long she'd been simply existing. She couldn't go back to the half life she'd been living since Harry died. Liz turned around and the edge of the pool dug into her ribs as she leaned forward, pausing inches from his mouth. "Alive," she murmured. And kissed him.

CHAPTER TWELVE

THE FEEL OF HIM was like coming home.

Shocked, Liz started to pull back, but Luke cupped her face in his hands and deepened the kiss. The flare of passion was instantaneous, searing. Her limbs grew heavy, her heartbeat rapid.

Desperately, she wrapped her arms around his neck, absorbing his vitality, needing it, needing him. She'd attributed their fiery lovemaking the other night to celibacy. Thought sex would calm down now and become manageable. Instead…

She broke the kiss. "We should talk about this first."

"I can multitask." Slowly, Luke peeled her wet swimsuit down to her waist, his intense gaze as effective as thirty minutes of foreplay with her late husband.

Shaken, Liz crossed her arms protectively

across her bare breasts. "Talk about how to manage this," she insisted.

Luke looked at her folded arms. "Is this leading up to domination fantasies?"

"No!"

"Hey, I'm open-minded." Even his tone was seductive. "I'll tie you up—you tie me up."

"No," she whispered, less convincingly.

His eyes darkened. "Liz…" Water spilled onto the pavers as he pulled her out of the pool and onto his lap. She didn't resist. His skin was warm and dry, his tongue wet and hot. Not a breath of air stirred the subtropical heat.

Her hands traced the contours of dense, supple muscle as his mouth closed on her breast and the rasp of his jaw on her chilled skin was a sensual torture.

Restlessly she repositioned herself to give him better access while another part of her brain whispered, *Rules!*

His hands skimmed her body, bypassing the swimsuit bunched at her waist to caress the sensitive skin of her inner thighs.

Dazed, Liz wondered if his bumblebee tie was handy for the tying-up part and the outrageous thought snapped her back into lucidity. She struggled upright. "We keep our affair secret," she insisted.

Luke slid a finger under the wet Lycra and she shivered under the light scrape of calluses across already her already swollen flesh. "I love your secrets," he said hoarsely and started to stroke.

Using every last ounce of willpower, she stilled his hand. "About the rules," she said desperately.

"I like to break them." Gently, Luke pushed her down onto the towels by the pool's edge, pulled off her swimsuit and replaced his fingers with his mouth.

Liz closed her eyes and the sun pulsed red on her lids, matching the throb of her blood. Red for stop, red for passion, red for a flagrant, addictive eroticism. The sun-baked tiles radiated heat through the damp, soft towel under her back.

Tension built until her whole body thrummed with it, until the plaintive cry of seagulls and the faint shouts of children playing in the lagoon faded. Until the world telescoped to what Luke was doing to her under the hot sun. But she couldn't lose control *here.*

Biting her lip, Liz opened her eyes. Reflected in the glass of the ranch sliders, a wanton sprawled half-naked on a crimson towel while a dark-haired man pleasured her. She gasped as her body convulsed.

When Liz came back to earth, her head was

cradled on Luke's muscled bicep and he was stroking her wet hair. "Okay?"

"No, dammit." She pushed up on one elbow. How dare he look like a cat, comfortably stretched in the sun when she needed a decompression chamber? "We're supposed to discuss rules *first*."

"No running with scissors?" Lightly he scratched her back. "No harming animals in our sexual experiments."

"You're not taking this seriously."

"I figured that was one of your rules."

She narrowed her eyes. Leaning forward, Liz used her tongue to capture the last water droplet, still sparkling on his navel. Under her lips, his muscle tensed. Emboldened, she followed the drops wherever they led.

They led down.

She made a leisurely exploration with her mouth before glancing up. The teasing light had left Luke's eyes, replaced by a savage hunger that reignited her own.

Wordlessly they stripped bare. Their damp bodies touched, skin drying quickly until they were sliding smoothly against each other, mouths and fingers exploring, instinctively avoiding the final joining. The sensual web spun tighter.

Rules. "At any time one of us can break it off with no hard—" Liz gasped as Luke moved between her legs.

"Hard?" His voice was gravel.

"Feelings…no feelings." Senses heightened, she could smell the freshly watered garden mixed with the jasmine and frangipani, the chlorine on her skin. It was too much. "Luke!"

He held himself above her on strong arms, magnificent and fierce, then his eyes cleared. "It's okay, Fred, I get it. No demands except sensual."

She took him into her body and watched his self-control fracture.

It made her lose her own.

MEN WERE THE ONES supposed to fall asleep straight after sex. But the mayor slumbered, sprawled in an untidy heap of limbs across his chest. Tenderly, Luke pushed back Liz's damp hair and her brow twitched in a momentary frown.

One arm holding her limp form in place, he reached behind him and carefully draped a towel over the chair so her face was in shade. Then he lay back, relaxed and curiously at peace.

The sun crept over the roofline, bringing welcome shade. Finger-combing the tangles in

Liz's hair, Luke thought lazily that he could stay like this forever. His hand stilled.

Carefully, he rolled the mayor onto her back, covered her with a towel and went to make them both breakfast.

"You look different."

Neville dropped the steaks on the barbecue and studied Liz through a haze of meat-sizzling smoke. "Happier."

"Of course she's happier. We're finally leading the polls." Kirsty patted her husband's rear as she carried a bowl of potato salad to the outdoor table where Harriet already sat in her high chair, gnawing on a chop bone.

"And less tense," Neville added thoughtfully.

Unable to bear his continued scrutiny, Liz snatched up a serviette and wiped away the flecks of greasy charcoal from Harriet's rosebud mouth. The baby growled and clutched her bone. "Mine! Iz!"

"Kirsty's right, it's been a good week." Liz hoped Nev attributed the flush in her cheeks to standing beside the barbecue. "Having the community groups endorsing my candidacy has made a real difference." It had been Luke's idea to approach them. "Whatever Snowy says, you're the one who's been working with them." And he'd been right.

"No, it's more than that." Nev turned the steaks. "You're getting regular—" Liz choked on her wine and started to cough, and Kirsty leaped forward to thump her on the back.

"Regular…?" Kirsty prompted her husband when Liz waved her off.

Liz stared at Neville though watering eyes. "Exercise," he finished, putting the steaks on a serving platter. "Haven't you noticed how toned she's getting?"

Kirsty stood back and took a critical look at Liz, then prodded her upper arm. "He's right. When on earth do you find the time…and what are you doing checking out your stepmother-in-law?"

"I'm a guy, we notice these things. And she's not my stepmother-in-law, she's my friend." Under his accountant's crewcut his dark blue eyes were kind.

"I need to be fit for the swim challenge," Liz managed to say.

"Well, I hope you don't go swimming alone." Kirsty handed her the green salad. "Damn, I forgot the dressing." She left the table and went inside.

Neville dished Liz a steak, passed it over. "That explains why I see the mayoral car parked in the cul-de-sac near the lagoon sometimes when I'm out jogging with the local running group."

She tried to think of something to say. Couldn't.

"Others in the club have noticed it, too…. Let me pour you some more wine."

Confused, Liz looked at her empty glass. She had no recollection of drinking it.

"You may not know this," Neville refilled his own glass, "but the salt in a sea breeze can cause rust even over short periods. Park a little farther back in Glendon Close."

"Nev…I…"

"To happiness." He tapped his glass to hers. "Now tell me if you think I've overcooked this steak."

Driving home later, Liz questioned her sanity. A thirty-five-year-old public servant needed a cat, not a sizzling affair.

The irresponsible part of her mind, the part that had hijacked Liz's brain lately, blew a raspberry.

Frankly, only a grown woman could handle an affair with a man like Luke. Remembering the kinky chess game they'd played last night, Liz nearly drove through a red light. In the nick of time, she slammed on her brakes and jolted back into the seat.

Another good reason to stop this madness.

Making love every night was suicidal given their crazy schedules. The light flashed green and she eased her foot off the brake. Yet she'd never been so full of energy. Tireless, if permanently light-headed.

And Luke's entrepreneurial expertise had proved an invaluable boon for her economic policy. "Oh, yeah," she mocked herself, "you're sacrificing yourself for your constituents."

Why couldn't she be serious about this? She was too giddy, too flippant, too…*reckless*. Even now, when Nev suspected.

And he doesn't *care*.

But Kirsty would. Which is why it was so important to…park where Nev suggested.

Oh, yeah, Lizzie, that's your solution.

She pulled into her driveway. What was wrong with an affair between two consenting adults who'd pre-agreed on the rules? As long as she didn't love Luke, she didn't have to feel guilty or disloyal.

Or end the affair.

LUKE SAT IN THE CAMP cafeteria playing Rock, Paper, Scissors with a table of eight-year-olds.

Moana was due in his office after the lunch break for another telling-off by a dork, as she called it. Over the past four days she'd been in his office five times.

She wanted to be sent home, her teachers wanted her sent home, the kids wanted her sent home. Something in Luke couldn't do it.

The eight-year-olds were all looking at him with dubious expressions. "You've done rock for the last five goes," one complained.

Luke unclenched his fist. "Sorry." He changed to paper and was promptly cut to pieces by four pairs of scissors. Mustering concentration, he managed to score a point.

The game had been one of Liz's many ideas when he'd admitted he was out of his depth with the kids. They liked it, too—probably because he was so bad at it. "So scissors beats rock right?"

"Noooooooo!" Five little kids rolled their eyes and giggled. Okay, maybe he played it up sometimes. Lately he'd found himself getting involved whenever he could spare the time. On a practical level he wasn't needed very often, but there was always a child dying to share his or her excitement—or hanging back, needing encouragement.

And then there was Moana.

Unconsciously, his fist curled back into rock and was promptly smothered by three sheets of exuberant paper. The lone scissors looked nervous, and Luke patted her shoulder. "The others have already shut me down. You're safe."

The bell rang and the noise level crescendoed as the kids scattered to their various activities. At the far table he saw Moana, a sullen blot on the landscape, sitting under Rosie's supervision.

"Okay, you two. Let's talk."

In his office, Luke pulled his chair around next to the couch and studied Moana for a moment. Under his scrutiny, her scowl grew blacker, too big for such a small face.

"Rosie, can you tell me what happened this morning?"

"We were riding bikes around the bike trail, the next thing I knew, Moana threw herself on Ryan and Cody and starting punching them. Moana admits she started it."

The girl gave her standard response. "This place sucks. I hate it and I want to go home."

Rosie looked at Luke and shrugged helplessly.

They knew home was subsidized housing in South Auckland with an exhausted solo mum who was raising six kids on a meager government benefit. Moana was the eldest and her mother's main helper.

He'd phoned Moana's mother last night and the child she'd described wasn't the sulky, mean one sitting in front of him. "Your mum really wants you to have a holiday, here," he said. "How do you think she'll feel if I send you home early?"

For a moment she didn't answer, then her eyes filled with tears. "Bad."

Rosie straightened in her seat. It was the first time Moana had shown an emotion other than anger.

"But they laughed at me, them other kids, because I can't ride a bike." Moana's scowl came back. "They said *everybody* knows how to ride a bike."

"Do you have a bike?"

She shook her head.

"So, why would you know how to ride one?"

"But *everybody* has a bike, even if it's old."

"The kids said that?" Rosie interjected.

Moana's answer was an angry sob.

"I never had a bike," said Luke.

"You're lying," the child accused him. "Everyone knows you're rich. You would'a had lots of bikes, hundreds even."

"Okay, I did get a bike when I was twelve," he conceded. "That was the year my swim coach fostered me into his family, which was much, much better than some old bike." *For a while.* "But you've had a family all along, haven't you? How many brothers and sisters do you have again?"

"Five."

"You're so lucky. You know, I think you have the most of any kid here."

"Joseph has six," Moana said. "*And* a bike."

"Yes, but Joseph is the youngest so he probably gets bossed around."

Moana brightened. "Yeah, he *does*."

"How about I take you out biking after dinner tonight," Rosie suggested. "Teach you when there's no one around?"

"Nah." The small shoulders slumped. "I got nothing to ride on at home." Fiercely, Moana knuckled her eyes dry. "Dad hit us a lot, but if he was still around at least we'd have stuff and not be freaks."

"One of my early foster dads smacked me around, too." Luke kept his delivery as casual as Moana's. "So I understand why your mum sent your dad away. She wanted to protect you kids. And it's better, isn't it, even if you have less money for things like bikes."

"Yeah, I guess," she conceded after a moment's thought. "Dad did break my arm once."

Rosie gasped and Luke sent her a warning glance.

"Tell you what. Let Rosie teach you to ride a bike and I'll buy you one to take home."

In the process of wiping her nose on her sleeve, Moana stopped. Stared. Then her mouth started trembling and she hurled herself at him.

Instinctively he stopped her with a hand on her thin shoulder. Then realizing his error, he offered her a handshake. "No big deal, hey?"

Confused, Moana shook it. Rosie caught the child in a bear hug. "Go join your group now. I'll be there in a minute." The kid ran as though she had wings on her feet.

For a minute the adults looked at each other silently.

"Why didn't I think of ringing her mother?" Rosie said.

"It wasn't my idea."

Liz had suggested it. Her influence was as pervasive as the fragrance of the port-wine magnolia outside the open window behind him. He no longer asked her to visit the camp, but her keen interest implied it wouldn't be long before she did.

Rosie stood to leave, then hesitated. "Did Social Services find out about that foster dad who hit you?"

"Yeah, they prosecuted." His mouth twisted. "Fortunately for both of us he died before I grew up." Seeing the sympathy on her face, he added briskly, "It's okay, Rosie. I got over it."

"Does running the camp help, Luke?"

He'd never dissected his philanthropy. As some of society's most vulnerable members, kids had seemed the obvious beneficiaries when he'd investigated setting up a charitable trust. Now Luke realized how personal his choice had been. "Yeah," he said slowly. "It does."

When Rosie had gone, Luke sat for a couple of minutes, thinking about Moana. He hadn't experiencing such a sense of achievement since he'd trail-blazed Triton Holdings with Jordan and Christian. He made a mental note to buy Liz some flowers as a thank-you and then grinned.

Somehow happiness had sneaked back into his life. He didn't trust it, he wouldn't rely on it—but he wasn't stupid enough to question it, either. He was simply going to enjoy it.

CHAPTER THIRTEEN

"HI THERE!"

He might not know the brunette standing on his doorstep with a vivacious smile and pink Vote Liz Light rosette, but Luke sure as hell recognized her baby.

Harriet looked up from her stroller and brightened. "Ook."

"I'm Kirsty Carrington," said her mother, "and I'm campaigning on behalf of Liz Light. Were you aware that she's restanding for the mayoralty?"

"Yeah, I'm a great supporter."

"Ook!" Harriet squirmed to get out.

"No, honey, stay there." Kirsty dipped into her bag, handed Harriet a carton of juice and Luke a flyer. "Then you'll be interested to read her policy manifesto." She handed over Liz's new pamphlet, the one he'd offered design advice on, but Luke couldn't concentrate because Harriet was looking at him with tragic brown eyes. Her lower lip started to tremble, and she began to wail.

"Oh, honey." Kirsty took her out. "Sorry," she said to Luke. "It's been a long morning." She set Harriet down and the child toddled over to Luke and grabbed his legs.

"Up."

With nothing for it, he swung her into his arms.

"That's amazing," Kirsty said. "She's usually wary of strangers." She stared at him, clearly impressed. "The rumors *are* true. Luke Carter is a babe magnet. I'm saying that because I have an ulterior motive in coming here."

"You do?" For a moment he thought Liz might have confided in her, but he dismissed the idea. She was paranoid about Harry's daughter finding out about them. Harriet wriggled to get down and Luke set her on her feet. Immediately she pushed through his legs and trotted into the house.

"Harriet!" called her mother. "Come back."

The tot answered her mother's summons by picking up speed.

Oh, *hell!* "I'll get her, you stay here."

Luke strode after Harriet, saw her bypass the lounge and disappear into the spare bedroom where the toys were. Glancing through the glass ranch sliders toward the inner courtyard, he saw the surface of the pool still rippling but no sign of wet footprints. Liz's lime-green bathing suit lay where he'd pitched it earlier, in a damp heap on the concrete pavers.

They'd been enjoying a nude swimming lesson when the doorbell rung and he'd told her to stop panicking and stay put while he got rid of the caller.

"Did you find her?" Kirsty's voice immediately behind him made Luke jump. A beaming Harriet toddled back into view holding the red ball. "How on earth did she know where to find that?"

"She must have seen it from the front door." Luke scooped up the baby, caught her mother by the elbow and started shepherding her out. He'd suddenly realized where Liz was.

"Nice pool. Oh!" Kirsty stopped dead. "Are these your swimming medals?" He still hadn't put them away since the wedding. They sat on the coffee table in the lounge, waiting to be polished and stored. "May I look?"

"Let me get them for you."

But she was already in the lounge. "Wow, I've always wanted to see one of these up close." Silently cursing, Luke followed her, positioning himself so that Kirsty had to face east, toward the sea views to talk to him. "They're amazing!"

Behind her, Liz's face broke the surface of the pool. She took a deep breath and went down again.

Harriet chortled "Iz." They'd played this game before.

"She's not here, honey," said Kirsty absently. She turned the medals over to read the backs. It seemed to take forever.

Luke waited until Liz came up for another breath. "I don't want to be rude but I've got a heap of work to do."

"Of course." Kirsty put the medals down.

Chortling, Harriet toddled over to the ranch sliders and banged on the glass. "Iz."

Luke tucked her under his arm like a rugby ball and headed toward the front door.

To his relief, Kirsty followed. "I'm sure you've heard about the Mayoral Swim-Safe Challenge."

"Once or twice."

"I know it's two days' notice, but would you consider shooting the starting gun? It would be such a coup to have an Olympian involved…for the kids," she added.

Luke had already intended to go. This way he'd

be close enough to give Liz a few words of encouragement. "Happy to."

"And Lizzy told me not to ask you." Kirsty's smile was triumphant. "She said you'd be too busy with the camp."

Uh-oh. He ran a hand through his hair. "Maybe I should check my schedule first." But this was an opportunity to do some community bonding in the wake of Wednesday's article.

An idea occurred to him. "Would the coordinator be open to some Camp Chance kids joining in?" Kirsty looked doubtful and he deftly turned the screws. "That would make it a lot easier for me to say yes."

She rallied. "The more the merrier."

After they'd left, Luke went back into the house and followed the wet footprints through the lounge to the bathroom door. It was locked.

"Do I need a password?" he asked through the keyhole.

The door flew open; Liz was already dressed. "This isn't funny, Luke. That was too close."

"Is telling her so bad?"

"Yes." Liz hunted for her shoes. "She wouldn't understand."

"She just asked me to get involved in the Mayoral

Swim-Safe Challenge." Watching her carefully, he caught the flicker of dismay in her dark brown eyes. "I was right. You don't want me to."

She stepped into her high heels. "It's safer if we avoid each other in public."

"As far as I know, wives aren't expected to throw themselves on their husband's funeral pyre in this country."

"You think I'm being silly. So does Neville… Kirsty's husband."

In front of the hall mirror, she rolled her hair into a French twist, caught it with a fancy clip. "I don't know how to explain it to people who weren't living here when Harry was alive. The town loved him. I mean, really loved him. Did you know there's even a statue of him planned for the botanical gardens? Seeing me play the merry widow…well, it won't wash, Luke. Especially when I'm playing with…" Her voice trailed off. Their eyes met in the mirror.

"Me," he finished.

She turned and stroked his arm. "Unfortunately the graffiti incident has stirred everybody up again."

A sense of unease temporarily diverted Luke from his personal concerns. "When I met you at the council building on Monday, I was dropping off another Resource Consents application. We want to use the camp for corporate team-building—in addition to its charitable use." He sketched in details of Camp Corporate. "How much opposition do you think we'll get?"

Liz stepped back. "The only reason council—and Harry—approved consent was because there was absolutely no commercial intent.... Now you're changing it?"

"Only because we have to reduce our dependance on fund-raising." Her expression worried him. "You think we're opening up a can of worms with this?" Shit. His instincts had told him there'd be trouble. "Obviously I'm not expecting Delores to support the idea."

"Not only Delores." Her face was pale under the makeup. "I can't support it either, Luke."

He stared at her. "You're kidding."

"No," she said quietly, "I'm not."

"But you support Camp Chance."

"Yes, I do. As it is." He hated it when she adopted her ice-maiden demeanor. "But turning it into a commercial enterprise, even if it's only part of the time…I don't know." She started to pace. "All the ecological considerations were based on three months of residential use a year. Now you're talking twice that."

He waved a dismissive hand. "We've done studies into all that. Additional impact will be minimal. Trust me, Camp Corporate won't compromise Beacon Bay's character."

She stiffened. "Are you telling me Triton had this in mind when you first applied?"

"No, I only got the idea when sponsorship started drying up. But all the research we did to get Camp Chance approved still applies. Of course, I'd prefer to wait until the kids camp is up and running properly, but the proposed district plan has torpedoed that idea."

He hesitated. "To be brutally honest, Liz, Camp Chance's future depends on it being self-funding. We need your support."

For a moment she wavered, then straightened her shoulders. "I'm sorry," she said in her best mayor's voice, "but Harry was unequivocally opposed to any commercial development of the foreshore. It was his line in the sand."

"I'm not asking Harry," he said slowly. "I'm asking you."

"How can I support something I know he was so adamantly opposed to? It would be disloyal."

Luke was sick of hearing about Harry. "What about your loyalty to me?"

Her mouth tightened. "My personal relationships have nothing to do with decisions I make as mayor."

"If that's true then why are you using your dead husband as a touchstone for every bloody decision?"

The ice-queen mask cracked. "At least I don't expect you to side with me just because we're sleeping together. Is that what this affair's all about?"

For a moment the accusation hung in the air like gun smoke. Then Luke said with dangerous quiet, "Is that really the man you think I am?"

The hurt in his expression steadied her. "No." Liz took a deep breath. "I'm sorry." How had conflict escalated so quickly between them? She and Harry had never fought. She didn't know she could get so wrought up.

Luke appeared similarly shell-shocked as he rubbed his hand over his face and gestured to a chair. "Let's talk about this."

"I'm already late for work." And she needed to regroup, process these churning emotions.

He glanced at his watch. "Hell. I've got a conference call in five minutes. Later then."

"Yes, but…I won't change my mind." Whatever her private qualms, she had to stay true to Harry's vision. Because as long as his legacy was alive, so in some vital way, was he.

Stony-faced, Luke led the way to the door.

Liz pulled out the set of house keys he'd given her and held them up, keeping her composure only by concentrating on the shiny metal. "I completely understand that this makes it impossible for you to give me further lessons." Obviously their affair was over. The ache of regret surprised her.

For a long moment there was silence, then with a pained sigh Luke closed her fingers over the keys. "Still trying to prove our relationship is dependent on your camp support, huh? I'm not falling for that trick." Astonished, Liz lifted her gaze to his. His humor was forced, so was his smile. It didn't matter. "I'll keep trying to change your mind, but it's lessons as usual."

As she continued to stare at him, a glimmer softened the impervious expression in his eyes. "But I'll probably play hard to get for a few days."

His generosity took her breath away, made Liz wish she could tell him what he wanted to hear. But she couldn't. "If you're sure?"

He still held her hand. "We're friends, aren't we?" he challenged her.

"Yes." Her fingers tightened on his. "We're friends."

"I'D LOVE TO KNOW who Luke Carter's sleeping with." Kirsty finally found a car park in the area cordoned off for Swim-Safe officials and swung her red Alfa Romeo into the tight space with a zippiness that made Liz clutch the dashboard.

"What makes you think he's sleeping with someone?" Her nerves were already shot without having to deal with this, too. She looked at the red and green pennants flapping in the breeze, the people swarming onto the beach, the children in their goggles and togs dragging bright towels—and her stomach lurched. Her shaky fingers fumbled with the catch on the seat belt. "It's jammed."

"I saw a discarded bathing suit lying by the pool. Female." Kirsty reached over and undid it.

"Maybe he's a cross-dresser."

"Yeah, and all the best-looking guys are gay. Not this one."

Last night he'd dropped into the council offices where Liz been working late and practically frogmarched her to her car. "Athletes need an early night before the big event," he'd insisted, then cut off her protests by pinning her against the civic building and kissing her senseless. "I think I'm ready to stop playing hard to get."

"It's only been twenty-four hours."

"I'm addicted." Liz knew exactly what he'd meant. He'd kissed her again, then reluctantly stepped away. "But tonight, Mayor Light, you need sleep, not sex. You've got a big day tomorrow."

Out of the car, it was thirty degrees Celsius. Shivering, Liz dragged her kit bag out of the boot. "Ohmigod, I forgot my goggles."

"No, you didn't," Kirsty said patiently. "They're around your neck. I've never seen you so nervous. You can swim, can't you?"

"Yes." *In a pool. Not in a choppy sea*. A gust of wind hit them as they walked onto the beach, throwing sand in Liz's eyes and making them water. She didn't stand a chance.

Officials with loudspeakers and reflective armbands milled among the crowd, and the kids participating had been corralled into a makeshift fence of fluttering yellow tape. Her legs felt as if they were sinking farther and farther into the sand.

"Look, there's Nev and Harriet," said Kirsty. Glancing at the base of the dunes, Liz saw Harriet, nearly obscured under a sun hat, digging clumsily in the sand with a red plastic spade. Nev waved. She could barely lift her hand to wave back. And she was expecting to swim with this arm? Panic broke through her dread.

Beside her, Kirsty prattled on. "I think his lover is local. There was no car parked in his driveway, so either it's a big secret or she lives within walking distance."

"Will you shut up about Luke Carter's lover!"

Kirsty stopped dead in her tracks. "Lizzy!"

Deep breaths, Liz told herself, deep breaths. "I'm sorry." Suddenly too hot, she unzipped her tracksuit jacket and stripped it off, bundled it into her carry bag, then took Kirsty by the arm. "The thing is, I'm not a *great* swimmer and I'm a little nervous." They drew closer to the starting line and Liz tightened her grip. "Humor me by talking about something else."

"I like your bathing suit," Kirsty said tentatively. "Is it new?"

She'd bought it to replace the one by the pool in case Kirsty had seen it. Luke had told her she was being paranoid. This one was red. Red was probably a shark's favorite color.

Across the sea of children Liz caught sight of Luke chatting to the organizers. If he was wrong about Kirsty seeing the swimsuit, he could be wrong about her being ready to do this.

"I'm sorry, but I have to say one other thing about Luke Carter," said Kirsty. "Hubba hubba."

He did look good in his ice-blue Camp Chance T-shirt teamed with black board shorts that exposed the solid muscle of his great legs, but right now Liz's strongest urge was to cut and run. Kirsty peeled her reluctant fingers from the sports bag and gently pushed her into the fray. "You'll be fine."

The children were wild with excitement. They jumped and pulled and chattered at her, all teeth and smiles. Liz automatically dispensed pats and words of encouragement, hearing nothing but the thundering of her heart.

Luke caught her by the hand and he pulled Liz into a circle of adults, squeezed her hand and let go.

SHE LOOKED so petrified, he ached to take her in his arms and reassure her that every athlete felt like this before a big event. For the first time, Luke felt the frustration of keeping their relationship secret.

They couldn't go on like this.

Over the next thirty minutes as he stood on the sidelines watching Liz shake hands, smile for the obligatory photos and interact with the excited young swimmers, he came to another realization. She was good at this. Very good.

Knowing how terrified she was about the swim, he could only marvel at how well Liz could still perform a mayor's primary function—building community. Somehow, after he'd introduced her to the camp kids, she managed to mix the shy newcomers with local children.

The ice-blue swimming caps of Camp Chance were now dotted among the crowd, instead of being clumped together in a defensive huddle.

"I hope you've done a head count." Frowning under an enormous straw sun hat, Delores Jackson came to stand beside him. "Remember, adequate supervision was one of the conditions of consent."

"It's a kids' camp not a high-security prison. And for the record, they're disadvantaged not delinquent." He'd been meaning to have a word with her since her quote in the *Chronicle*. "When are you going to give me a break?"

"When I can trust you to keep to the rules."

Rules. Despite his irritation, Luke smiled. "People need to feel part of the community before they buy into its rules, Delores. Did you ever consider that?"

They spent the next five minutes in a heated philosophical discussion. If so much didn't ride on her influence he might have enjoyed it. With her active intelligence, she should be running a business, he reflected, instead of minding everyone else's under the guise of the Residents and Rate-payers Association.

"What did you do?" he asked abruptly. "Before you became a witch."

"I was a dental nurse for forty-two years."

"So torturing poor kids is a calling, then?"

Her eyes sparkled. "If only they'd all had your big mouth…my job would have been so much easier. Your charges have better manners than you do."

That surprised him. "You mean you've actually been talking to some of them?"

"Mr. Carter?" An official hurried over. "We're ready to start."

LIZ FELT rather than saw Luke approach because she couldn't tear her gaze from the orange marker buoys parallel to the beach, bobbing in and out of the whitecaps. "I think they're drifting farther away," she muttered.

He squeezed her shoulder. "A couple of kids from Camp Chance will be swimming with you, Mayor Light. They're a little timid in the water and I was hoping you'd keep an eye on them for me."

Liz's attention snapped back to him. Was he crazy?

Luke beckoned the kids forward. "Meet Moana and Jayden."

Automatically, Liz shook hands. The girl, pre-adolescent and slight, looked as though she'd be swept out on the tide; the older boy, maybe fourteen, was twice Liz's weight. "I don't think—"

"A couple of tips, guys," Luke said to the kids, and she shut up and listened. "This isn't a race, so relax. Take your time and have fun."

Liz reswallowed her breakfast.

"With the choppy water you might have to slow down and take more breaths or even lift your arms and body farther out of the water on each stroke." Luke demonstrated. Desperately, Liz copied every move. "Water's probably going to get in your mouth but there's no need to panic. Simply blow it out during your stroke and then take a breath on the next one. Okay?"

Liz realized all three were staring at her and the penny dropped. She wasn't their lifeguard; these kids were hers. And by the anxious looks on their faces they were taking that responsibility very seriously. She couldn't let them carry that burden, so she croaked, "No sweat."

"You guys go in the first shot of the starter gun. The other kids will follow you after four minutes."

Her chilled fingers wrestling with her goggles, Liz nodded.

"You can do it," he murmured. "And if all else fails, walk."

Her panic eased slightly but the sound of the starter's gun still had the punch of a heart attack. Her smile set like rigor mortis, Liz jogged into the sea, Jayden and Moana kicking up spray beside her. She'd expected the water to be as icy as her blood; instead it closed around her as benignly as a warm bath.

Luke was right—she could do this.

"Don't worry," whispered Moana, behind goggles that took up half her face. "We'll look after you." With an encouraging smile she dived into the water like a fish.

Jayden looked after her wistfully, but said to Liz, "You can go first."

Taking a deep breath, Liz started to swim, trying to ignore the push and pull of the surface chop. It was difficult—she adjusted her stroke, turned her head for a gasp of air—but not impossible. With grim concentration, she counted ten strokes, then lifted her head to sight the marker. Adrenaline had given her power and it was much closer than she'd expected.

Rounding the second buoy, she choked on a

mouthful of seawater and had to stop and tread water while she coughed it out. A banshee cheer went up from the beach and the shoreline exploded into white water as a hundred kids hurtled into the sea. "Yikes."

Jayden's blond head surfaced beside her. "You got a cramp?"

Water streamed off Moana's ice-blue swimming cap as she powered back toward them. "What's wrong?"

"Nothing." As long as they stayed ahead of the hordes. "Race you," Liz invited. Water slapped her across the face as the two kids kicked away from her at speed. Carefully, Liz followed in their wake, so intent on coordinating her strokes and breathing that her hand hit the seabed before she realized she was in knee-deep water.

Feeling like a fool and grinning like an idiot, she stood up and dragged off her goggles, instinctively searching for Luke in the cheering crowd.

He stood among the kids and counselors of Camp Chance, feet slightly apart, arms folded, watching her. Ray-Bans shielded his expression but she could sense his pride, as warm as the sun on her back, could read his delight in the wide smile, a slash of white against his tanned face.

This feeling, so rusty, so lovely…what was it? For a minute Liz couldn't identify it because it was tangled with the euphoria, the sense of achievement.

Then she did.

CHAPTER FOURTEEN

LUKE HADN'T SEEN Liz in two days and he was getting withdrawal symptoms. One hand on the steering wheel, he massaged the back of his neck with the other. She could defuse the day's tensions with a touch.

In his driveway, he switched off the 4WD's engine and stared at his big, empty house. So the challenge was over, so she didn't need swimming lessons, so the elections were eleven days away and she had to prepare for the public meeting next Tuesday.

All good reasons, but his instincts told him they were excuses. Thoughtfully, he got out of the car, checking his mobile for messages. None from Liz. He'd sensed wariness, even a formality, in her attitude after the swim and in their two brief phone-calls since. Something was bothering her, and he wanted to know what it was.

Maybe it would be third time lucky. He brought up her number. About to push Send, Luke paused. Was Liz turning into an obsession? Aborting the call, he picked up the courier package sitting on his doorstep and let himself into the house.

This was the perfect opportunity to regain some perspective on their affair. And if it turned out that he'd served his purpose and she didn't need him anymore, well, easy come, easy go.

He dropped his keys on the bench and ripped open the envelope. His thoughts elsewhere, it took Luke a moment to focus on the contents. He hadn't expected to feel anything and the pain took him by surprise.

Pouring himself a straight bourbon, he sat on the deck in the gathering twilight for an hour, then, unable to stand his thoughts any longer, pushed redial.

LIZ HADN'T INTENDED to answer the phone. This was a special night and she'd already put on Harry's favorite music—Vivaldi's *Four Seasons*—and settled herself on her bed with the photo albums. Except…what if it was Kirsty calling to share memories?

"Hello?" she said.

"Liz? It's Luke."

"Hi."

"Have you eaten?"

She had to smile. He was always trying to feed her. "No, not yet."

"There's a casserole in the freezer that Jord made last time he was here. Can I tempt you?"

Too much. "I can't tonight."

"Look outside the window, Fred." Though it was after eight, the setting sun had turned the sky into a watercolor sunset of delicate pinks and violets. The estuary, on full tide, twisted like a melted rainbow through the mangroves. "See what you're missing by working?"

Liz turned away from the view. "It's not work, it's…something else."

"Why are you avoiding me?"

She gave him part of the truth. "It's Harry's birthday and I wasn't planning on seeing anyone."

"We don't have to have sex. Let's raise a toast to his memory…I've got a ghost that needs laying to rest myself."

"No." Harry and Luke had to be kept separate. "I'd rather…not."

There was a brief pause. "Sorry for being so slow. I've got my diary here, so let's mark those important dates now. The first time you and Harry met. The first time you kissed…made love. Your wedding anniversary—"

"The day he died. December third."

There was a tense silence. "I'm sorry." Luke's tone was no longer savage, but strained and tired. "My divorce came through today. I guess I'm jealous of your perfect love."

Now she understood his persistence. "Luke, I—"

"It's all right, Liz. I understand. Enjoy your special evening." He hung up.

With mixed emotions, Liz replaced the receiver. Dammit, this was *their* time, hers and Harry's. Luke was already impinging on her thoughts too much. This was one of only two days in the year she devoted to Harry—his birthday and the anniversary of his death.

Determinedly she stuck to her rituals—lighting candles, opening a bottle of Harry's favorite wine, settling on the bed with her albums. But the sense of sanctity was gone.

Staring at a picture of herself and Harry on holiday in Sydney, she found herself worrying about Luke. "He's a big boy," she told her husband's image. "He can take care of himself."

In fact, Luke insisted on it…which made the hint of desperation in his invitation more unnerving. "Dammit, he's ruining our evening."

In the photo, Harry smiled.

"Well, if you're going to be this casual about it, I might as well tell you…I could be falling in love with him. Which is the *last* thing he'd want."

Harry's smile didn't waver.

"*I* don't want to." Her eyes filled with tears. "Oh, my darling, I don't. I need to be safe. Please come back to me."

But as with all the other pleas she'd made over the last twenty-seven months, nothing happened. Drying her eyes, Liz went downstairs with the wine bottle and found a cork, then picked up her bag and took both out to her car.

She might not be able to ease her own misery, but at least she could alleviate someone else's.

LUKE OPENED the door with a glass in his hand. "Oh, hell," he said.

His shirt was unbuttoned, his eyes were slightly bloodshot and his hair looked as if he'd been clutching it.

"I see I've got some catching up to do." Liz handed him the bottle as she passed.

He closed the door and followed her into the lounge. "What are you doing here?"

"We're friends, aren't we?"

Luke passed a hand over his eyes. "Yeah, we're friends, but—"

"No buts—pour me a glass of wine." She added curiously, "So how drunk are you?"

His grin was rueful. "Enough to wish you weren't here."

She walked into the stark lounge. "How about we sit outside?"

"Yeah, I look a lot better in the dark." He pointed—not to the pool courtyard—but to the deck on the ocean side. "I'll get a glass."

She followed him as far as the dining room, shifting newspapers on the table to make room for her handbag. Luke's Olympic medals fell to the floor, landing on the wood with a clang. "Oh, look what I've done." Horrified, Liz crouched to pick up the tangle of ribbons. "I'm so sorry."

From the kitchen, he glanced over the breakfast bar. "Don't worry about it. They'll be fine."

"Did you leave them out for cleaning?" Carefully, Liz returned them to the table. God knows they needed it. The kids at the wedding had really given them a hard time. Looking more closely, she saw the dullness on the metal was longstanding. "You know I use Metalson on the mayoral chain. I'll give you some."

"Sure." Luke pulled a wineglass out of the cupboard and held it up to the light. Even from here, Liz could see the dust.

Maybe it was painful for him to remember his glory days. She touched the discs with reverence. "You must miss it sometimes."

Rinsing the glass under the tap, he snorted. "Which part? The relentless training schedule that meant I didn't date until I was eighteen? The public adulation that turned to disgust whenever I didn't place? Or maybe the weight of carrying other people's dreams? My coach—"

The glass, clinking against the sink, stopped him. "God, I'm getting maudlin, aren't I?" He checked it for cracks then added lightly, "Swimming got me a scholarship to university. I'll always be grateful for that." Reaching for a tea towel, he started drying the glass. "Go sit down, I'll be there in a minute."

Liz took the hint.

Outside, she found a deck chair between a half-empty liquor bottle and his divorce papers. She picked up the bottle and sniffed. Bourbon.

"Bring Coke," she called. If Luke wanted to drown his sorrows, that was fine, but he should probably slow down.

Pulling up another deck chair, Liz made it comfortable with cushions. Beyond the dunes, she could hear the sibilant whisper of the waves, mere meters away but, from where she sat, she could only get a glimpse of the moon-bright sea. He was a man who guarded his privacy.

A shadow fell on the light spilling onto the deck. Luke padded out and handed her a glass of wine. Splashing Coke into his drink, he raised his glass. "To?"

"Surviving," she said.

"Good choice." They chinked glasses and he sat down. "I'm over her, you know," he said conversationally.

Liz sipped her wine; it was tart and cold on her tongue. Lime, green apple and a hint of grassy herbs.

"It's the messy way Amanda did it I'm still bitter about," he said. "I had to find out she'd left me for 'true love' through the tabloids."

"Dignified goodbyes—we all want them," she said slowly. "My last words to Harry were 'Don't forget the Slug Slam.' We had a snail infestation in the canna lilies and he was driving past a garden center."

"I like that," he said. "Love *should* be domestic and comfortable and something you can take for granted."

Except Harry had never come home. "You can never take love for granted."

There was a small movement on the dunes, and for a moment a rabbit stared at them.

"Amanda and I never had those kinds of conversations. Truth is, I sucked at marriage. Maybe the capacity for intimacy was conditioned out of me in the children's home before I got fostered." He swirled the ice cubes in his glass. "No, it was probably earlier when my mother left me there." Because there wasn't a trace of self-pity in his voice, it took a moment for Liz to register what he'd said. She turned her head to stare at him.

"I can't blame Amanda for having an affair," he continued reflectively. "Hell, if she hadn't publicized it, I'd even be glad she found someone who could make her happy."

"That's a good attitude," she managed to say.

"Except it also lets me off the hook." Luke refilled her glass, topped up his own with Coke. "I don't have to feel guilty."

"Just because you couldn't love Amanda—who doesn't sound very lovable, I have to say—doesn't mean you're incapable of the emotion. I know it sounds like a cliché, but you haven't met the one."

Maybe it was the earnestness in her voice, maybe it was her profile, pale and beautiful and sad under the moonlight. Maybe it was the hot burn of bourbon that finally made Luke hear what his heart had been telling him ever since the wedding. Oh. Shit.

"Tell me about Harry," he said, because he had to know if he had a chance with her.

She did.

And he didn't.

He went back on the bourbon.

THE MOON ON HIS FACE woke Luke at two in the morning. He vaguely remembered Liz putting him to bed, fully clothed. With a raging thirst he went to the bathroom and drank from the tap, great gulps of water, then filled the sink and dunked his head.

It wasn't enough, so he stripped and showered, letting the water pummel every screaming nerve. *No. No. No.*

"Luke, are you okay?"

Wearing one of his T-shirts, Liz peered anxiously through the steamed glass. "You're still here," he said.

"I'd drunk too much to drive. I'm in the spare room."

Of course she was, Luke thought sourly. Because she didn't want to have sex on her late husband's birthday.

Except it wasn't Harry's birthday anymore.

Turning off the shower, he stepped out and started drying himself down with a towel. Slowly.

Liz took a step back but her gaze stayed exactly where it was. On his body. Under the thin cotton of the T-shirt, her nipples pebbled. The camp's logo rose and fell with her quickening breath.

"Sweltering in here, isn't it?" she said and shoved open a window. Luke grinned. The steam spiraled lazily into the night.

As she turned back, he lifted his arms and started toweling his hair dry. Her gaze fastened on his biceps and she moistened her lips.

Luke clenched his fists in the towel to accentuate the muscle. "Are you hungry, Fred?" he asked innocently, then had to drop the towel to cover himself. Watching her dark eyes melt always made him hard. Anger flashed through his need and the fun suddenly went out of the game. He'd given her too much power.

Liz's expression grew wary. "We never did get around to eating."

Luke knotted the towel around his waist. He had to start practicing self-control where this woman was concerned. "Let me get some clothes on and I'll meet you in the kitchen."

As he pulled on a T-shirt and jeans in his bedroom, Luke decided he needed to kill these new feelings before he slept with her again. He was a realist, so it shouldn't be difficult.

In the kitchen, he stuck the Pyrex dish, still dewy from being defrosted, into the microwave, then buttered some bread rolls. Liz arrived fully dressed and dropped her car keys casually on the counter. He scowled.

"I'm probably okay to drive home after we've eaten," she said awkwardly.

"Go now if you want to."

Her color heightened. "It's you who doesn't want me here."

Her perceptiveness annoyed him. "Of course I bloody do," he snarled, lifting the lid. Not chicken casserole but pumpkin soup.

"Why are you angry with me?"

For once Luke's customary honesty deserted him. "What makes you think that?" He poured the golden broth into a couple of mugs and carried them over. "Here."

He held out a mug. Liz sniffed and looked down, then recoiled as though he were offering her a rattlesnake.

"What?" he asked impatiently.

Liz started to choke, her throat closing up. She hated that smell, hated where it took her.

Back to that foster home. Back to herself as a child, the smothered gagging as she forced herself to spoon her plate clean.

"For God's sake, Liz, what is it?" Still holding the mug, Luke came closer.

Clapping a hand over her nose and mouth, Liz stumbled to the doors and threw them open. She sucked in deep breaths but the stench lingered in the heavy humidity. "Liz?" Luke said beside her and her nausea became panic. Seizing the mug from his hand, she hurled it up and into the dunes. Under the security lights, the soup fell in an arc that splattered across the pale sand; the mug landed with a thud. She started to shake.

Luke pushed her down into a deck chair. "Stay here while I get rid of the rest."

Teeth rattling like castanets, Liz sat hugging herself. She flinched when another mug was thrust under her nose. "Brandy," Luke said. "Drink it."

Her eyes watered as she choked it down, but the alcohol stripped the last cloying trace of pumpkin from the back of her throat. Luke picked her up and carried her to bed then wrapped himself around her. The last chill of shock worked its way through her bones.

Completely empty, Liz cried. As helplessly as when she'd first heard of Harry's death. Cried until her nose streamed, her eyes swelled and her head ached.

And while she sobbed, Luke soothed her with nonsense words of comfort, stroking her head and shoulders. Their bodies grew hot and sweaty under the blankets; he kicked them off, but he never stopped holding her.

Her fingers dug into his back, but Liz couldn't make herself let go. When her sobs abated to intermittent spasms, she gasped. "This…is…silly. No one hurt me. Nothing…to complain about… No one abused me."

It broke his heart.

"But did anyone hold you?" Against his chest she shook her head, not making a sound now, even as another deluge of hot tears scalded his skin. "Did anyone love you?"

In the midst of shaking her head, she paused. "Yes. Harry."

No, he could never compete.

She pulled away a little, looked up at him with eyes that were red and swollen. "Who hugged you?"

His throat tightened. "I'm not sensitive like you."

Her hold tightened until he thought his bones would crack. "Tell me."

"I was six when my mother put me in care, saying she'd come back for me. She never did." Liz's hair tickled his nose as he shrugged. "Probably never intended to."

"You can't know that for sure. Maybe her life was hell, maybe she was working to better it before she came and got you. Maybe…"

His nonchalance deserted him. "I waited at the door of that home every Christmas and birthday for three years on the strength of maybes." He'd never told anyone this before, not even Jordan and Christian. "Then she died, and I finally had peace."

"Oh, Luke."

"No pity, Liz."

"Go to hell," she said and kissed him.

Luke pulled away. She was taking him from a

man who felt too little to a man who felt too much. "Let me get you a washcloth for your face. A glass of water."

"I'm sorry, I must taste like the Dead Sea... No, don't turn on the light."

When his emotions were under control, Luke went back. He stood and watched her as she gulped down the water. Her wedding ring glinted in the light from the hallway.

Luke took the empty glass, chill against his fingers, and placed it on the bedside table. Still standing, he asked, "Why were you in care?" In silence, he waited while Liz fought through her reluctance.

"My father was a single parent. He tried, but he worked long hours at a poorly paid job and my child care was...erratic. Social Welfare intervened when I was five. I didn't live with him again—he died when I was seven."

"And the soup?"

Unconsciously she pulled up the sheet. "One of my foster parents was hot on self-discipline. My aversion to pumpkin soup was something she thought I should master." Liz laughed weakly. "I guess...the lesson wore off."

It was the laugh that got Luke. He knew this

woman, knew what had shaped her, as it had shaped him, knew her strengths and weaknesses as a result. It was like being given X-ray vision into another person's soul.

And it was impossible to withhold the compassion he rarely allowed himself. Impossible not to admire what she'd overcome…without any of the riders he put on his own achievements. They had been soldiers in the same war.

He'd come to think of himself as invulnerable, but Luke realized suddenly he was helpless against loving her.

Taking the washcloth out of the bowl of water, he sat on the edge of the bed and passed it lightly over her pale, exhausted face and tear-swollen eyes.

Liz sighed as she exposed her neck to the wonderful coldness.

"Lie down."

Obediently, she slid down the headboard. Tomorrow she knew she'd be ashamed about this; right now she needed his comfort.

Luke's fingers moved to the buttons of her rumpled blouse, the zip of her skirt. Gently he stripped her naked. She closed her eyes as the cloth traced her collarbone, her shoulders, her arms and hands.

Heard the trickle of water as he rinsed and squeezed the cloth, then felt the weight of it on her breasts and stomach, skin tingling in the wake of its delicious trailing coolness. Her nipples peaked; Luke's hand stilled.

Then the sheet was being pulled up and Liz felt the brush of a kiss on her bare shoulder. "Get some sleep."

Opening her eyes, she grabbed his leg. "Don't go."

Under her hand the muscle tensed, but his voice was calm. "If that's what you want."

She expected him to undress, but Luke only removed his T-shirt before he lay down beside her, on top of the sheet. The embarrassment Liz expected to feel tomorrow arrived early.

"You know I'll go." She pushed back the sheet. "It's dawn soon and if I'm home I'll—"

He rolled over to trap her body under his. "Don't be hurt." Gently, he pushed a loose strand of hair behind her ear.

"If this is pity, get off me."

Luke nuzzled her neck, following the sensitive sinew down to where it joined her shoulders. "God help me, it's not."

Liz opened her mouth to ask what he meant

and he kissed her in a way he never had before, a kiss both tender and fierce.

His erection pressed hard and hot through his jeans, the rough denim scratched her inner thighs, he smelled of clean sweat and aroused male and his hands were rough-skinned on her sensitized skin. But his kisses were heartbreakingly sweet.

Their lovemaking had always been passionate, intensely physical, now every stroke of his tongue was laced with a dangerous tenderness that both stirred and scared her.

Lightly, she raked her nails across his back, trying to change the mood. But his lips still on hers, Luke captured her hands and held them by her sides while he continued his exquisite seduction.

There was something intensely erotic about being kissed so gently by a big, powerful man while she lay naked under his half-dressed body, helpless to touch him.

And though she knew it was dangerous, Liz found herself responding in kind, beguiled by this precarious, poignant intimacy. The world reduced to their intertwined fingers, Luke's weight pressing her body into the mattress and his mouth making tender love to hers.

At some point he released her hands: reverently

she traced the smooth muscle of his back, then unfastened his jeans and pushed them down, solely focused on drawing him closer.

She cried out as he entered her, painstakingly gentle even in this, and wrapped her legs around his body, needing the feel of him, skin to skin.

With every stroke, he kissed her, his tongue mimicking the movements of his body.

Liz gripped Luke's shoulders, trying to control it, but her orgasm was a shattering of boundaries.

Still he hadn't finished, intensifying his strokes, bringing her to another climax, and taking her with him into oblivion.

Afterward they held each other in silence. It was the sense of rightness that triggered Liz's insight and made her suddenly stiffen.

Luke was the lover in her dream.

CHAPTER FIFTEEN

LIZ MOVED restlessly in his arms, and Luke let her go. It really was too hot to lie together but—he pulled her back for a lingering kiss—he wanted to savor this rare intimacy while he could.

Abruptly, Liz ended the kiss. "I should go."

He glanced at the luminous green dial on the bedside clock. "It's only five. Stay another thirty minutes."

She rolled away from his embrace. "No!" Sitting on the bed with her back to him, she added more calmly, "I...I have a lot to do today."

"Then of course you must go," he said evenly. He turned on the light to see her face. He refused to believe that their recent lovemaking had changed nothing, meant nothing.

Liz blinked and avoided his gaze. "I'll shower when I get home."

Propping himself up on an elbow, Luke watched

her dress with her usual brisk efficiency. He'd never been invited to the house she'd lived in with Harry. But then affairs didn't take place on hallowed ground.

He'd always considered his ability to confront unpleasant truths a strength; now Luke hated it. With his history, loving a woman who couldn't love him back was emotional suicide. He had to give her up while he still had self-respect to cushion the fall.

While she used the bathroom, he dressed and found her bag and shoes. "Here you go."

"Thanks." Her smile was tight; her eyes looked right through him. In silence, they walked to the door. Outside, the dawn sky drizzled rain. It was still dark enough to trigger the security lights.

"Liz, I think we should stop sleeping together," he said quietly. Now he had her full attention. Luke watched the emotions chase across her face— shock, disbelief, regret. But he also saw the relief. His heart started to bleed. "With the swim challenge over, you need to concentrate on the election."

She turned away to look at the rain. Under the lights, the tiny drops glittered in her hair. "We always knew this affair was a temporary arrangement," she said.

Fool that he was, part of him had still hoped she'd change the rules. "Plus, I've been neglecting Triton business since the kids arrived. I need to catch up."

She gave him a searching, anxious look. "But we'll still be friends?"

He took an umbrella off one of the coat hooks in the hall and handed it to her. "Of course."

Numbly, Liz took it. An honest man was always so bad at lying. "That's settled then." She touched her lips lightly to his, resisting the urge to cling. All she'd wanted was space to think. Of course he'd ended it. After her performance last night, it had stopped being fun.

As she walked blindly down the driveway, Liz realized she'd had a narrow escape from complete humiliation.

"Liz." On a heart-skip of hope, she swung around. "The umbrella," he reminded her.

The rain had got harder without her even noticing. With a bright smile, she fumbled with the mechanism and hid her stricken expression under the canopy of emerald green. "Silly me."

"WELL, I MUST SAY it's nice to finally be singing from the same hymnbook." But a slight frown drew Delores's eyebrows together as she stood up, and Liz realized the older woman would have preferred a battle.

Rising from her chair, she reflected that politics made strange bedfellows. "Mr. Carter's proposal still has to be judged on its merits through the planning department."

"Yes, yes." Delores picked up her handbag. "But if none of the mayoral or council candidates support the proposal, it will be much harder to push through."

About to open her office door, Liz paused. "Snowy's made his decision then?"

"He knows which side his bread is buttered on. And when I make it an election issue, the other candidates will follow suit."

Liz was careful not to flag her disquiet. "Is that necessary?" she asked with a smile.

Delores gave her an incredulous look. "The only time public opinion *has* any power is in an election year. We'd be crazy not to use it to kill further development. And to think I was starting to soften toward that man." The familiar martial light kindled in her eyes. "I'm sure Luke Carter was planning this all along. Well, he'll soon learn he can't play me for a fool."

"I know that was never his in—"

"Of course it was. As if delinquents aren't bad enough, now he's expecting Beacon Bay to endure corporate shenanigans and hordes of yuppies. Anyway, Elizabeth, I'm glad you've joined us. I'd been hearing rumors."

Liz's hand tightened on the door handle. "Rumors?"

Delores paused beside her. "That you support the camp."

"I do support Camp Chance—" Liz opened the door "—but, Harry...I mean, *I'm* against any corporate use."

"Well, you're doing the right thing now at least" was the grudging reply.

Then why did she feel so guilty? Closing the door against the persistent scent of lilac, Liz leaned against it with a frown. Since Luke's new plans had become public knowledge her stand had been vindicated time and time again.

Without any prompting, everyone—from the tea lady to Kirsty—had volunteered his or her opinion that Harry wouldn't have countenanced Camp Corporate. Even Luke's supporters on council took Liz's opposition for granted.

The only reason she'd told Delores her decision was to take the heat out of the issue. Let Luke's proposal take its chances with everyone else's. At the very least she could give him a level playing field. Instead, Delores considered it a mandate for war.

Frowning, Liz looked at the phone, wondering if she should ring the camp and warn Luke. *Are you sure you're not looking for an excuse to talk to him?*

Okay, she missed him. But—Liz gathered her things and left her office—he didn't miss her. He hadn't called once. So that was that and she could concentrate on winning the election. Ahead in the polls now by a good margin, all she had to do was hold a steady course and the job stayed hers.

In the lift, Liz stared at her reflection in the steel doors. So why did she look so sad? Yes, there was Luke and getting over her crush on him. It relieved her to name it.

Obviously she wasn't cut out for casual and that was all Luke had wanted. And really, that was all she'd wanted, too. She was never going to love someone as much as she loved Harry because the pain that came with the goodbye…

Oh, God. Liz pressed her fingers into her eyelids. *Get over it. He doesn't want you.*

But her unhappiness was about more than losing Luke. For the first time in her life she was at odds with Harry. Having Delores in her office this afternoon only intensified Liz's conviction that—this time—she was on the wrong side. And it was driving her crazy.

In the foyer, she nodded a distracted goodbye to Mary at reception.

"Give that gorgeous baby a kiss for me."

"I will."

Outside, Liz pulled Harriet's car seat out of the trunk and fixed it in place in the backseat. She was picking her darling up from crèche. That would cheer her up. They would go to the beach, make a sand castle, swim… She found an upbeat song on the radio and turned it up loud. Enjoy all the things that children who were loved and nurtured could take for granted.

The camp's future depends on it being self-funded.

Oh, hell. Liz leaned her forehead against the steering wheel.

"I'm sorry, Harry," she whispered. "But I'm pulling rank on you."

"WHAT DO YOU *mean* you're supporting Camp Corporate?"

Kirsty dropped the flannel she was using to wash Harriet's back. It landed in the bubbles with a splash and set the family of rubber ducks bobbing frantically. Harriet grabbed Mother Duck and tried to chew her head off.

Sitting on the bath's edge, Liz hoped it wasn't a sign. "When I first decided to run for mayor I made myself a promise. To be uncompromising in my values and flexible in my views. I'm allowed to change my mind, Kirsty."

"But you know Dad was absolutely opposed to any commercial use of the beachfront."

"This is a conscience call for me." Liz hesitated. Keeping her childhood private was too engrained to surrender the secret lightly. "For the charity to prosper, it needs its own income."

Retrieving the flannel, Kirsty vigorously scrubbed her daughter's back. "They should have thought of that before they started."

Harriet gave a squeal of noisy protest; Liz took over the flannel and the washing. "With twenty-twenty hindsight, I'm sure they would have located Camp Chance somewhere else." *And I wouldn't have met Luke.* Despite her misery, something in her protested.

Kirsty's mouth tightened. "Well, I'm disappointed, Lizzy, and I know Dad is turning in his grave."

Liz was trying not to dwell on that. Gently, she washed Harriet's face. "It's me I have to live with."

"Okay, let's leave the personal issues aside for a minute. Sticking your neck out on a controversial issue a week before an election is crazy. As your campaign manager I have to advise against it."

"Someone has to counter Delores Jackson's tirades with reasoned argument before she does too much damage. And how much credibility would I have if I wait to show my hand after the election? None."

"Who cares?" Leaning forward, Kirsty pulled the plug on Harriet. The squeal of draining water was the only way to get her out of the bath. "At least you'll be elected."

Liz lifted the clamoring baby free and rescued Mother Duck from the plug monster.

"*Now* who's turning Harry in his grave?"

"Fine," said Kirsty grimly, handing Liz a towel. "But don't say I didn't warn you."

For the first time since Liz had started having weekly playdates with Harriet, her stepdaughter didn't ask her to stay for dinner.

BUT IT WAS Liz's heart that turned over when Luke called her name three nights later. She was approaching the hall where the mayoral candidates were due to summarize their policies for the last time before Saturday's election.

"You're back from Auckland," she said inanely, then blushed. Now he'd know she'd been keeping tabs on him.

"An hour ago. Rosie said you're supporting Camp Corporate."

Of course, he wasn't here for her. "That's right."

"What changed your mind?"

"My conscience. I couldn't spend time with Harriet without thinking about kids who don't have her advantages." Dammit, he shouldn't be looking at her like that, when he didn't mean it. Briskly she added, "But wait until you've seen my conditions before you get too excited. There are a lot of controls on the use of that land."

"I have, and I'm still grateful. We all are… Christian, Jordan, the camp counselors." The gratitude in his voice stirred her emotions, all too close to the surface.

"Don't. If I get teary-eyed my mascara will run and then what will my constituents think?" She grimaced. "And I don't want to embarrass you again."

"What do you mean?" His tone was sharp.

Wishing she'd never raised the subject, Liz shrugged. "Being so needy the other night. No wonder you—" She stopped herself in the nick of time, glanced at her watch. "I have to go."

As she turned away, he caught her arm in a firm grip. "Is *that* why you think I ended it?" When she hesitated, he said, almost to himself, "Of course it is. Hell, I was so intent on saving my pride, I didn't even consider how lousy the timing was."

Saving pride seemed like a fine idea to Liz. With a tight smile, she freed her arm. "I shouldn't have brought it up. Forget it."

As she hurried away, his voice followed her. "I ended it because I can't share you with Harry anymore, Liz. It's not good for me."

She turned around and stared at him. What did he mean by that…? Did he…? Could he?

"*There* you are." Glancing over her shoulder, Liz saw Kirsty hurrying toward her from the hall. "You're needed inside. Hi, Luke. Hmm, I'm not sure I should be talking to you. You do know Camp Corporate is jeopardizing Lizzy's reelection?"

"She's exaggerating," Liz's brain was still reeling. "Can we talk later?"

Luke's gaze sharpened. "Is there more to say?"

Was there? She took a deep breath. "Yes."

He nodded. "I'll find you."

Liz followed Kirsty through the side door into the hall. "Liz!" Jo Swann beckoned to her from the stage. The publisher was emcee tonight. "You're speaking after Snowy." He was already at the podium, lowering the microphone. Beyond him, the hall was slowly filling with people.

Liz took her seat beside Delores and scanned her notes, trying to focus. The old lady ignored her but, since changing her stance, Liz was getting used to disapproval. Unfortunately Snowy had also become rabid in his opposition.

When Liz had tackled him about the camp privately, he'd been blunt. "Given your lead in the polls, I needed a controversial issue to bring some parity into the race. It could have been anything, Liz, but by changing your stance on the camp so close to the election, you handed me this one on a plate."

She hadn't repeated that conversation to Kirsty; their relationship was strained enough already. Liz turned into Snowy's PowerPoint presentation and frowned.

"If council approves Camp Corporate," he said, "any Tom, Dick or developer will be able to push through foreshore projects because a precedent has been set."

She raised a hand. "I'm sorry to interrupt but that's incorrect and Deputy Mayor Patterson knows it." Ignoring Snowy, she looked to Jo. "May I clarify the situation?"

Receiving a nod of assent, Liz outlined the council regulations that would prevent rampant development and listed the exceptional conditions that made the charity unique.

Her gaze, calm and reassuring, swept across the crowd. "Contrary to what some of the Letters to the Editor in the *Beacon Bay Chronicle* have implied this week, I have no intention of jumping into bed with big business or allowing a string of high-rises to be built along the waterfront."

Snowy gave a bark of laughter. "My God, what an apt analogy."

"Excuse me?"

"I have some pertinent information on this topic that I'd like to present if I may, Madame Chair."

Jo frowned. "You sound as if we're in a court-room, Snowy."

"And so we are—in the court of public opinion." He nodded to the assistant running his PowerPoint presentation. "As you know," he said, "we've had cameras installed outside council offices in an attempt to stop a graffiti problem."

"A problem that began well before Camp Chance opened," interrupted Liz, "so if you're trying to make a connection between the recent tagging and camp kids—"

She caught her breath on a gasp as a still came into focus on the screen, a gasp lost in a collective one from the crowd.

"Taken on the eve of the Mayoral Swim-Safe Challenge, this shot is from video footage too steamy to replay in full," Snowy said. Liz stared at the picture of herself locked in Luke's embrace. Turning her head, she glimpsed amusement, embarrassment and disapproval in the crowd—but it was Kirsty's reaction she searched for.

Her stepdaughter was staring fixedly at the screen, her expression stricken.

Liz turned on Snowy. "How *dare* you violate my privacy like this. What possible justification could you have?"

"Public interest," he shot back. "So, Mayor Light, the exceptional conditions you mentioned in relation to Camp Corporate… Is one of them the fact that you're sleeping with the developer?"

CHAPTER SIXTEEN

IN THE HUSH that followed Snowy's question, Luke stood up, clapping slowly. "Bravo. You really must join the amateur dramatics society, Snowy, when you fail to win the mayoralty. You've got a real talent."

"Even so, he raises an excellent point," said Jo Swann. "How long have you two been—"

Blushing to the roots of her hair, Liz cut her off. "I can assure you that my support of Camp Chance predates our personal relationship."

Ignoring her interruption, Luke said smoothly, "Obviously facts will carry more weight than assurances. We're more than happy to answer any questions you have." Telling the truth would remove any hint of illicitness from the scandal Snowy was intent on brewing. "We've been dating a few weeks."

But wily bastard that he was, Snowy concentrated on Liz. "I'm not talking about your general endorsement of the camp, but your particular support of Camp Corporate. On Friday you told Delores Jackson you were against it, on Monday you'd changed your mind. How do you explain that?"

Again Luke answered. "Before you develop your conspiracy theory, Snowy, let's clarify a few facts, shall we? The late mayor endorsed Camp Chance and his successor has done the same. Liz Light has never been involved in planning meetings, a fact that can be independently verified. And her decision to support Camp Corporate simply means that she'll use her public profile to voice the interests of those who don't have a voice—the kids who'll benefit by the money it brings in."

The whispers faded as people started to listen.

Jo frowned. "If everything is aboveboard, why did you hide your liaison?"

Luke looked at Liz. Only she could answer that one.

"In light of my late husband's profile…in light of my own…I wanted some part of my life to stay private." But she knew—as Luke did not—that a lot of people in Beacon Bay were going to be disappointed in her. "I can only reiterate that my decision to support Camp Corporate had nothing to do with Luke Carter."

Except, looking into Luke's gray eyes telegraphing his support, Liz realized that wasn't entirely true. If it weren't for him, she would never have reconciled with her past. Never challenged herself to step out from Harry's shadow.

Flustered, she looked at Kirsty, who read Liz's doubt and sprang to her feet. "Of course he's influenced you," she accused. "Everybody knows Dad would never have permitted commercial activity on the foreshore. Admit it, Lizzy, you know that, too."

She couldn't lie. "It's true that Harry wouldn't have supported—" The rest of her words were lost in the noise from the crowd. It seemed everyone had an opinion that needed expressing.

In the ensuing uproar, she watched Kirsty gather her things. Ignoring those trying to talk to her, Liz hurried off the stage.

Luke stopped her at the bottom of the stairs. "Go back and stand your ground. You can talk to Kirsty later."

"Our affair has jeopardized everything I care about."

"Why are you acting guilty? You know we've done nothing wrong."

"You've done nothing wrong…I—"

She broke off as Kirsty marched past. "Stop! We need to talk."

Ignoring her, Kirsty shoved through the double doors leading to the car park. "Wait here," Liz said to Luke, and ran after her.

"All that talk of a conscience vote was a lie," Kirsty said over her shoulder. "How could you, Lizzy? How could you betray Dad's memory, not just privately, but politically?"

"You're wrong, Kirsty. No one influenced my decision, not even your father. And my relationship with Luke was already over when I changed my mind."

Kirsty stopped. "So it didn't mean anything?"

As she hesitated, her daughter-in-law's expression hardened.

Liz panicked. "No."

"You know what?" Kirsty tore off her campaign button and threw it on the ground. "That only makes your disloyalty worse."

"We'll talk when you've calmed down," Liz called after her. Then she'd tell Kirsty everything—about her childhood, about her complicated feelings for Luke Carter.

With a sigh, Liz turned around and froze. Luke

stood there. For a moment she saw her anguish reflected in his expression, then his eyes steeled to winter gray. "*Now* there's nothing more to say." He turned on his heel.

Liz let him go. She'd betrayed him, she'd betrayed Harry and she'd ruined everything that was lovely in both relationships. She deserved to be alone.

Somehow she gathered the nerve to go back, but Jo had managed to restore order and move the meeting along. Delores had taken her turn at the podium and by her strident tone, intended holding the floor for a while.

Liz hesitated at the side of the stage and stared at her empty chair, brightly lit by floodlights. What was she going to say? Her emotions were in turmoil, her mind blank with shock.

As she stepped forward, Jo caught sight of her and left the stage, grabbing Liz by the arm and steering her back behind the curtain. "Not a good idea. Emotions are running high and too many people have seen your campaign manager quit." Her tone was cool.

"I have to fix this," said Liz. "For everybody."

"Well, you've got guts, I'll give you that." Jo let go of Liz's arm. "But if I were you, I'd regroup first. I think everyone was ready to give you the benefit of the doubt," she added. "But by publicly admitting you're acting against their favorite mayor's wishes, then having his daughter question your ethics…I'm afraid you're screwed. You should have…" Her voice trailed off.

"Lied?" Liz smiled faintly. "Let's just enjoy the irony, shall we?"

For a long moment the two women stared at each other. "Don't give up," Jo said. "We need people like you in local government."

"I wouldn't give Snowy the satisfaction." But it was empty bravado. He'd beaten her and he knew it. Across the stage their eyes met. Smiling, he mouthed, "It's not personal, it's politics."

"You're right," she said to Jo, fighting down her rage. "I won't make any headway tonight and I need to prepare. What's the hall's availability?"

Intrigued, Jo checked the schedule. "Thursday's the only night free."

Two days before the election. Who the hell was she kidding? Liz lifted her chin. "I'll take it."

"YOU GUYS SHOULD be collecting your bags," Luke called across Camp Chance's sports field. "The bus is nearly ready to leave."

The cluster of kids conspiring at the tree line

behind the goalpost broke apart. Five voices rose in a crescendo as each vied to be heard.

"We're chasing a bird—"

"It's a seagull, dummy."

"His wing's tangled in netting but he won't let us catch him."

Luke put his hands over his ears. "No wonder, with that racket. Haven't you ever heard of commando tactics?"

Immediately they quieted to a reverential hush, as round-eyed, they awaited instructions. He gestured them into a huddle around him. "The important thing about being a commando is working together to sneak up on your prey. Where's the bird?"

Moana gestured to the newly planted trees skirting the playing field.

"Okay, I need you to fan out behind the trees and flush it out onto the field. I'll take it from there. Mo, you stay in case I need your help."

As they waited, Moana studied him, her dark eyes troubled. "You're sad."

"You're all going home," he said lightly. "I'll miss you." The first camp had been a great success. He wondered how many more Triton could sustain.

"Nah, you won't. 'Specially not me."

"I'll miss you the most." He ruffled her hair. "So guess you had a good time after all, huh?"

Her thin shoulder lifted in an insouciant shrug. "It was all right. I'm coming back next year," she added anxiously, in case she'd taken her cool too far.

Even if the camp was still here, he wouldn't be. "I'm glad." All the local support, so carefully built up over the previous weeks, had dried up in the wake of Tuesday's meeting. All because he'd committed the cardinal sin of getting romantically involved with Harry Light's widow. He'd jeopardized the camp's future for a woman who said their relationship had meant nothing. Sad didn't even begin to cover how he was feeling.

"I've come for that tour," said Liz quietly behind them.

Moana's face lit up. "Hi, Liz!"

Luke didn't turn around. "Ask Rosie to take you. I'm rescuing a bird."

"Can I help?"

"No." Out of the corner of his eye Luke saw Moana staring at him and added reluctantly, "We're fine. Thanks."

Behind him Liz murmured, "You're not making this easy."

His anger reached flashpoint. He'd let down his guard, and she'd inflicted a terminal wound. The Band-Aid of an apology wasn't going to fix this. And she wanted it easy?

He turned and glared at her, ignoring the fact that she looked like hell. "Then how about we make this effortless and fast-forward to the goodbye?"

Liz winced but held her ground. The bird squawked onto the field, one wing raised, the other trailing behind. Luke pulled off his T-shirt and with two quick steps had the gull wrapped snugly.

Through the cloth he felt its thinness; it hadn't eaten for a while. "Hold him, Mo, while I check the wing."

But Moana had retreated about twenty meters. Wordlessly Liz took the bird. It gave her hands a perfunctory peck before sinking its head into its shoulders, resigned.

"I came to camp because you won't answer my messages," she said in a low voice. "That alone must tell you how desperate I am. Please, Luke, let me explain."

"I'm bored with this subject, let's change it." He peeled the cloth away from the seagull's body.

"Okay." The pleading note had left her voice. "The night your divorce papers came through, you were talking about your swimming career. What were you going to say about your coach?"

He didn't flinch from the challenge. "He wasn't happy when I opted for early retirement and we grew apart."

"But…" She stared at him. "Wasn't he also your foster dad?"

The kids arrived, clamoring to see, so they crouched down. Moana tugged his arm. "What's wrong with the bird?"

"His wing's caught in a piece of fishing net— just as you guys told me. There's a hook under the skin as well, that's why he hasn't pulled it off."

Liz was so close, he could smell her vanilla perfume, mixed with her own subtle scent. With a deft twist, Luke removed the hook from the wing. The seagull blinked. "If you have to do something painful, make it quick." Deliberately, he pinned Liz's gaze. "Don't draw things out."

She swallowed.

Carefully, he started untangling the rest of the netting. "I hear Snowy's taken the lead."

She didn't flinch, either. "It's not over until the last vote has been counted." Even in his anger, Luke felt a flash of pride in her courage. "And there's still the meeting tonight," she added, "to set the record straight."

"I'll be there if that's what you're worried about. In public, we present a unified front."

In a low voice she said, "You know that's not why I'm here."

He concentrated on the task. "My fingers are too big to tease this knot out…any of you kids want to try?"

"Touch a bird? No way."

"It might peck me."

"What if he dumps on my hand? He's probably already done it in your T-shirt."

Liz gave him the seagull. "I'll do it." As she bent over the bird cupped in his hands, her hair trailed over his forearms in strands of blond silk. The kids edged closer again, their breath tickling Luke's bare shoulders as they strained to look.

There were memories in his life that Luke could evoke with all senses, and suddenly he knew this would be one of them. Crouching with the sun on his back, the new-mown grass fragrant in his nostrils, he closed his eyes, this moment so intensely tangled with life and inexplicable longing, it hurt. There was nowhere he would rather be right now than here with these kids and this woman saving an injured bird.

Liz stepped back. "Done."

Luke set the bird on the ground and gently unwrapped it. The seagull staggered forward, flapped its wings to steady itself, orange feet skittering down the field. "Fly," encouraged the children. "Fly! Fly!"

The gull stopped. "It needs to get used to the idea," said Liz. "We can wait."

Careless of her suit, she sat on the field, cross-legged; the kids followed her lead. They all looked expectantly toward the bird, and Luke felt a curious ache under his ribs. Their patience had so much faith. "And if it won't?" he murmured so only Liz could hear.

The bird flew. Just like that. Yelling, the kids chased its shadow down the field.

Liz screened her eyes against the sun, still following the seagull's flight, and he had to ask, "Have you sorted things out with Kirsty?"

"She won't talk to me unless I withdraw my support of Camp Corporate—as Harry would have wanted."

Luke remembered that Kirsty had held a grudge over the lifetime of Liz's marriage, and frowned. "But you'll still get access to Harriet?"

"Neville's trying to talk her into it, but…" Her voice trailed off. With jerky movements, she brushed grass clippings off her clothes.

His unease deepened. "C'mon, guys," he yelled, "you've got a bus to catch." They ran ahead, while he followed with Liz. "Are you saying that supporting Camp Corporate could cost you not just your job, but Harry's family?"

"It's not your problem." Liz quickened her pace and pulled ahead. "It's mine." He'd always enjoyed the mayor's brisk stride and her body's no-nonsense focus on reaching her destination. Today she walked as if hunted, with her head bowed, clasping her wrist.

Inside him, something crumbled.

She had no one left on her side. He was no different from Kirsty with her emotional blackmail or those in the community expecting Liz to act like a saintly hologram of Harry Light.

"Withdraw your support," he said curtly, catching her up. "You probably can't retain the mayoralty at this point but you can keep Harriet."

They'd reached the camp's front entrance. She stopped, dazed. "But this camp's future—"

"Is my problem, not yours." Screw it, he'd sell his share of the business if he needed to, to keep Camp Chance going. All these people, demanding

Liz be what they needed her to be. He couldn't be another one of them. "Do what you have to do, Liz. For once, put yourself first."

She took a deep, shuddering breath. "Luke, about what you overheard—"

"Forget it."

"I was lying when I said you didn't matter." Her voice was tight, almost breathless. "You do…too much."

Always the damn qualifier. Luke had quit competitive swimming when he stopped winning. Coming second wasn't in his nature. "I'm moving back to Auckland after the election."

"Oh." She went very still.

"Christian and Jordan have been agitating for their turn, and given recent events I'll probably do more harm than good by staying."

"If that's what you want."

He couldn't get what he wanted. "Listen, I have to go," he said roughly. "Get these kids organized. Rosie!" he called. "If you've finished saying goodbye, show the mayor around the place, will you?"

"If now's not a good time—" Liz began.

"It's fine. See you at the meeting." He left her standing there.

At the bus he shook every kid's hand as they prepared to embark. "Joey, good luck with the rugby trials next week…. Donna, remember what I said about handling your brother…" If his heart would up and die he could cope, but the death throes were driving him insane.

He held out his hand to Moana.

"You're weird," she said and hugged him.

For a moment Luke couldn't speak. "Next year you might even be bigger than your attitude, Mo," he said in a husky voice.

Halfway up the bus stairs, Moana stopped and hollered to the kids still waiting to board. "Hey everyone, Luke wants hugs." With a cheeky smile, she disappeared.

That kid was always going to get the last word.

But after another dozen hugs, Luke felt as though he might live.

CHAPTER SEVENTEEN

CAMP CHANCE HAD BEEN inspiring.

Later that afternoon Liz walked along the shoreline, clutching her shoes in one hand.

Even though she knew a man like Luke wouldn't build anything but the best, it had always been seeing the kids in the camp environment that Liz had dreaded most. She'd been terrified of catching a glimpse of hopelessness, of fear...of lost expressions in their faces.

While she'd been heartened by the camp kids she'd met at the swim, it hadn't been enough to prompt a visit. When Liz had been young, all the confident kids had been paraded on the home's public outings—it was good politics. And Luke had professionals running Camp Chance.

The incoming waves hissed up the sand, then relentlessly dragged it away under her feet, forcing her to higher ground.

But she'd seen every kid as they clambered into the bus and Beth Sloane hadn't been reflected in a single happy face. Closing her eyes, Liz took a deep breath and let her childhood go.

There were still other things to let go, but she wasn't ready.

She opened her eyes and started walking again, faster now. Farther along the beach, a sand castle, dappled with sea foam, sagged into the swirl of water. Liz stopped and watched it disappear.

What should she do? Harry would have been able to tell her. And that was partly what troubled her. Had he always guided her or had she canonized him after he died? The real man was lost to her; all Liz had was memory now, uncertain and frighteningly selective.

Climbing to the top of one of the dunes, she sat and stared blankly at the horizon. In a few hours she'd be standing on a podium fighting, not only for her political life, but also for Camp Chance's future. Kirsty would be there, waiting to hear where Liz's loyalties lay.

Was keeping Kirsty in her life worth ditching her integrity?

As Liz agonized, a child's chatter pierced her reverie. A young woman power walked along the beach, her dark ponytail swinging with every stride. A young boy followed in her footsteps, dragging a long stick behind him. He stopped then, ditching the stick, bent to pick up a starfish.

"Mum, look what I found."

His mother turned, but kept walking backward. "C'mon, Brett," she coaxed. "Remember our game?"

Clutching his new treasure, the boy went back to stepping in her larger footprints, his short legs straining with the effort.

When they were out of sight, Liz resumed her walk, pausing next to the imprint of small bare feet in the tread of a larger sports shoe. On impulse she hunkered down to trace it with her fingers. Who cared about integrity when the alternative was losing Harriet?

She picked up the stick the boy had discarded and wrote the only absolute truth she knew in the wet sand, where the waves would soon obliterate it.

I love Luke.

A wave swept over the message, then receded, leaving the words fainter but still readable. Like a feeling that couldn't be erased. Liz walked on.

As much as she'd adored Harry, her love had always had a reverential quality. He was the one who first saw Beth Sloane as she longed to be. Special. With his unswerving devotion, he'd made Liz feel safe but—she acknowledged the truth— he'd never made her feel needed.

Luke needed her.

His eyes had given him away after she'd told Kirsty their affair hadn't meant anything. He loved her and now he was protecting himself and Liz was letting him because she had choices to make— hard choices.

Luke had told her to put herself first, even when her decision had the potential to hurt the camp's future…and his. As strong as Harry was, Luke was stronger. Yes, she loved him, but how would Kirsty react to *that?*

Liz realized she was matching her stride to the existing tracks and stopped. Hadn't she been doing this since Harry died? Walking in his shoes. On the other hand, her troubles had only begun since she'd started going her own way.

Her eyes burned. Independence had a price.

She remembered the words carved into the front entrance of Camp Chance and its promise to the kids who came there. "I believe in you," she recited in a low voice. "I have faith in you. I know you can handle it." There were other affirmations—about being cared for, listened to, about being valuable. Liz recited them all, then turned for home.

In her bedroom, she got Harry's old sweater out of the wardrobe and buried her face in it, her decision made.

LOOKING OUT across the packed hall, Liz cleared her throat. The sound reverberated through the microphone. A bad start. To her left, Snowy sat back with a smile.

She straightened her shoulders, stopped playing with her wedding ring. "Snowy Patterson accused me of having a conflict of interest…he was right." Murmurs broke out around the hall. "The truth is, I never really wanted to support Camp Chance— even when Harry did—because it reminded me too much of where I'd come from."

Quietly, Liz outlined her history, her voice growing in power as she became caught up in the need to make these people understand. "Projects like Camp Chance need a generosity of spirit—the same spirit that made me choose Beacon Bay as a refuge all those years ago. I won't believe we've lost that."

Luke stood at the back, wearing one of her campaign T-shirts. For a moment their eyes met, then Liz returned her attention to the crowd. "There's been a lot of conflict over the site, conflict that's taken the focus away from what Luke Carter and the other trustees are trying to achieve for those children. Whether I win a second term or not I think it's time for Beacon Bay to decide what kind of community we want to be. A place that posts a No Trespass sign or a town that says, Welcome, Friend."

Near the front, Kirsty sat tight-lipped with her arms folded. "I thought long and hard about going against Harry's wishes and it wasn't easy for me. You know how we felt about each other..." Her voice broke. "And I know how Beacon Bay felt about him."

Luke couldn't stand any more.

Slipping out through a side door, he jammed his fists in his pockets and strode back along the beachfront toward his house. Enough.

There was a fine line between selflessness and masochism and he'd just crossed it.

Pulling his cell phone out of his jeans he rang Christian. He'd never asked a favor in his life; he asked it now.

"Yeah, Jordan and I can step in earlier with the camp." Luke was grateful that Christian didn't mention that they'd been trying to share the load for weeks. "You want to talk about this?"

"Not unless you're a ghost buster," he said bleakly.

OUT OF THE CORNER of her eye, Liz saw Luke leave but it didn't worry her. There'd be time later to go after what she wanted. "One of the things I admired most about Harry," she continued, "was that he had the courage of his convictions. Yes, in this case, his convictions differ from mine. But this is a conscience vote for me and I make no apology for it."

She glanced at Snowy. "I believe people should always come first, and if you reelect me, they will. Thank you."

Liz stepped back from the microphone. The sound of her heels on the floorboards echoed through the silent hall as she walked back to her seat.

The applause started, slow at first, growing in volume until it swelled through the hall and carried her back to her chair wearing a smile so big, it made her cheeks ache. One good speech wouldn't be enough to swing the election in her favor, but hopefully she'd changed enough minds tonight to make a positive difference for the camp.

Delores Jackson sailed up to the microphone,

but it was a full minute before she could make herself heard.

After the meeting ended, she separated Liz from a herd of well-wishers with the skill of a cattle rustler. "You should be courting me." For once her voice was pitched low, and Liz had to strain to hear over the clatter of two hundred people filing out of the hall. "I have enough supporters to be the kingmaker in a tight race, should I decide to concede before the election."

"Wait a minute." Liz narrowed her eyes. "Holding the balance of power has been your intention all along, hasn't it?"

"I know I'm too strident to stand a chance of winning, but I couldn't have the wrong person in the job."

Some of Liz's elation dissipated. "You mean me."

More people came over to shake Liz's hand and Delores waited until they'd moved on. "I've never approved of your blind devotion to Harry's causes," she continued, "but tonight you proved that you're your own woman." The old lady stuck out her hand. "Integrity will always come first with me."

Astonished, Liz took the soft, wrinkled fingers with the iron grip. "And Camp Corporate?"

"If the conditions on development prove as

stringent as you say they are…maybe. But tell that man of yours I'll be watching his every move like a hawk."

Liz smiled. "I will." Behind Delores, she saw Kirsty struggling toward them against the outgoing tide of people, and her pulse kicked up a notch.

Kirsty tapped Delores on the shoulder. "Mind if Lizzy and I talk in private?"

The old lady turned around. "It won't do you any good. I'll find out anyway."

"You didn't know about Luke and Liz," Kirsty retorted.

"Who says I didn't?" With that cryptic remark, Delores left.

Liz ventured a tentative smile; Kirsty didn't return it. "You're replacing Dad with Luke, aren't you?"

For a moment Liz didn't answer. "If something happened to Harriet could you replace her with another child?"

"Of course not!"

"The people you love aren't replaceable, Kirsty—which is why I don't want to lose you, too." Liz hesitated. "But you need to accept Luke."

Kirsty pulled a face. "Dammit, you and Nev are expecting me to do the right thing, aren't you?"

"Yes." Liz's voice broke. "After all, you are Harry Light's daughter.

"I hate it when you play that card."

Liz opened her arms. "Still family?"

Kirsty blinked furiously. "Okay, but no hugs or you'll make me cry."

Liz hugged her anyway.

LUKE WASN'T PLEASED to see her.

Euphoric after her evening's successes, Liz hadn't expected the man she intended spending the rest of her life with to look at her as though she was selling something he didn't want to buy.

Particularly when it was herself.

With a sinking feeling, she remembered he'd never articulated his love. Maybe she'd taken too much for granted. "I know it's late," she began awkwardly, "but I thought you'd like to know that it went well. In fact I'll probably win the—" Behind him, she noticed two bags lined up in the hall. "You're not leaving?"

"I told you I was moving back to Auckland."

"But not tonight." The sinking feeling bounced off the bottom of Liz's stomach and started its ascent as panic. "What about us?"

"We'll always be friends."

Liz pushed him inside, shut the door and leaned against it. "You can't go. I love you."

"I know you do—but not enough. In your heart, Harry will always come first."

Liz steered him as far away from the door as possible, outside onto the sea deck where her panic could take wing. "Let's talk about this."

"It won't do any good, Liz." Under the bright moon Luke's expression looked even more remote as he folded his arms. "As the years go by, Harry will go from being a great guy to sainthood in your memory. Hell, he's already halfway there. A flesh-and-blood man can't compete with that."

"It isn't a competition and I can't pretend I didn't love him."

"Which is why I'm not asking you to."

She started to feel sick. "When Harry died I swore I wouldn't let anyone get so close again. That's why I kept pretending you didn't matter, but it was only pretense, Luke."

"I know bereavement," he said. "My mother abandoned me, my wife divorced me and the only father figure I ever had—my coach—severed our relationship when I retired early from competitive swimming. But I got over it."

"Now who's pretending?"

He scowled and looked away. "Be honest, Liz, half your heart will always be buried in a grave with Harry."

She scrambled for the words that would convince him he was wrong. "We cremated him." Those weren't them.

"Uh-huh. Where are his ashes?"

"We're waiting for his brother to come back from overseas before we scatter them…. What?" She was losing him and she couldn't seem to stop it. "Luke, I haven't got them in some sort of shrine at home." Only hours earlier, she'd put Harry's sweater in a clothing bin and said her last goodbye.

"I wouldn't know, I've never been invited there."

"Then let's go now."

Liz only realized she was gripping his forearms when he gently broke free of her hold. "It can't work, Liz."

And suddenly she understood. "Harry's not the real problem, is he? You're using him as an excuse. I hurt you and it made you realize how vulnerable you are. What's really going on is that the guy with intimacy issues is getting cold feet."

He didn't answer, but the grimness of his features told her she was right. Except she didn't want to be right.

"You want promises, Luke? You want guarantees? I can't give you any. At some point, love requires a leap of faith."

For a moment, his mask slipped and Liz saw the child he'd once been in all his aching vulnerability. Saw how much she was asking of a man who'd survived by safeguarding his emotions. "One day," he said carefully, "you'll find another Harry."

If Luke was going to make the right decision she had to help him. "I don't want another Harry. I want you." Liz started to strip.

He stopped her. "Sex won't solve anything."

"Good—" she shoved his hand away and kept pulling her clothes off "—because I'm not offering any."

When she was down to bra and pants, Liz grabbed a handful of Luke's shirt and hauled him closer. "Forget the leap of faith. I'm base-jumping from Everest." Releasing him, she walked toward the sea.

Torn between conflicting emotions, Luke watched Liz disappear over the top of the sand dune. He reached the top of the dune in time to see her striding into the moonlit sea.

"What the hell are you doing?"

"Drowning. Unless you save me."

"What the—I taught you to swim, remember!"

She didn't answer, simply threw herself into the next wave and began a slow, careful crawl toward the horizon.

Exasperated, Luke bellowed, "This is crazy!"

She swam out twenty-five meters, fifty. Stopped.

He always knew she'd turn around. Instead she treaded water and yelled, "Remember I loved you!" And began swimming again. A wisp of cloud covered the moon; for a moment Luke lost sight of her and his heart lurched. Then the moon reappeared and he saw the pale blur of her head.

Okay, she could swim, but not *that* far. And not in deep water.

Luke raced back to the deck for a life preserver but all he could find was one of Harriet's water toys. Then he kicked off his trousers, hauled off his shirt and dived into the sea. Powering through the swell, he silently swore, twice raising his head to sight her. By the time he reached Liz, she'd stopped swimming and was weakly treading water.

In his relief, Luke almost lifted her airborne. "What the *hell* do you think you're playing at?" With his free hand, he shoved the pink noodle at her.

But Liz wouldn't take it. "Is that a yes?"

Forcibly, Luke wrapped her arms around the long bendy noodle and started kicking toward shore, still too shaken to do more than rant. "You realize this is the second time I've had to save you?"

"You're wrong, I'm saving you—" they picked up speed as Liz started to kick, too "—from making the biggest mistake of your life. You're stuck with me, Luke. And Beacon Bay. I don't let go of the people I love." A lilt of laughter entered her voice. "Haven't I just spent the past two years hanging on to Harry?"

"I can't believe you think this was funny."

"Stop being a coward and jump, dammit."

"Easy for you to say, you've done this before."

"No," she said. "I haven't. I've never loved anyone the way I love you."

For a moment Luke stopped kicking. "You're mad," he said. "Insane. It'll probably come out in our kids."

Liz started to cry. They were close enough to shore to stand up, so he hauled her close, tossed the noodle aside and started kissing her, tasting tears and sea. "I love you…God, Liz, I love you so much."

Their kisses deepened, hot and salty and full of raw need. He skimmed his hands over her body, sleek and wet, barely covered. Liz hitched her arms around his neck and wrapped her legs around his waist. As he reached around to unfasten her bra, a wave crashed into them, knocking them over in a tumble of surf. They surfaced laughing.

"This always works so much better in the movies."

She pulled him into the shallows. "Let's try this on dry land."

On the deck, he caught her hand. "Are you sure, Liz?"

Cupping his face, she kissed him. "I'll take my chances." Her lips curved in a smile that was pure Fred. "And remember, I only wanted you for your body, anyway."

EPILOGUE

It WAS GALA DAY at Camp Chance, and Jordan King's long hair and Christian Kelly's Ferrari had been attracting almost as much attention as the stalls and activities, the most popular of which—Super Soak a Politician—had raised over twenty-five hundred dollars.

But right now, all eyes were on the friendly football game between the Camp Chance Raiders captained by Luke Carter and made up of trustees, staff and kids, against the Beacon Bay Butt-kickers.

Also known as Citizens Caning, the team led by recently reelected mayor, Liz Light, was primarily made up age-challenged councillors and ratepayers who were as surprised as anyone to find themselves leading the game six-two.

Particularly when they hadn't scored a goal.

Amid a howl of protests from the Raiders at the announcement, Luke approached the referee, who sat on the sidelines in an armchair, with the rule-book in her lap. "I think you'll find—once again—that was *our* goal, Delores," he said.

"I'll just check." A twinkle in her eye, she beckoned over her two linesmen. "Ladies, they're disputing the score again."

Kezia Kelly jogged over, her pigtails bouncing. Her mischievous expression offset the authority of her official uniform of green shorts, T-shirt and long socks. "Actually, Delores, I think the score is fifteen love."

"Oh, Jeez! Reinforcements!" Luke yelled, and Christian and Jordan joined him.

"No, Kez, you're wrong." Fellow linesman Kate Brogan-King, the baby bulge under her green shirt making her look like another football, waddled over. "You're thinking tennis. In soccer, a try is worth five points. So the Beacon Bay Butt-kickers lead by ten-two."

The three men looked at one another. "That's *rugby*, Kate," Luke said in a controlled voice. "In *football* we score a *goal* and a *goal* is worth one point."

"For the hundredth time," Christian added with exaggerated patience, "That's *our* goal there—" he pointed in a direction and obediently everyone looked "—and that's *their* goal at the other end of the field."

"The ball went into our damn goal," roared Jordan. "End of story."

"They're arguing with you again, ref," Liz said behind them. "Send 'em all to the sin bin."

"You know damn well sin bins only apply in rugby and to our bedroom, Fred." Spinning to face his wife, Luke caught Liz's wink to the other women. "Wait a minute. This is a conspiracy, isn't it?"

Delores frowned. "Ten minutes in the sin bin for questioning the referee's integrity. The rest of you back on the field, if you don't want to join him."

Everyone scattered. So much for loyalty. Resigned, Luke collapsed on the grass next to Delores. "My big mistake was giving you an open invitation to snoop around camp."

And next week, construction would start on Camp Corporate's dorm, which meant they'd be seeing even more of her.

"If you don't mind, big mouth, I'm trying to referee a game here."

"Sure you are—Jord, kids on the pitch!"

Jordan scooped up Harriet and Maddie, just as Christian kicked the ball to him. With a toddler on each hip, each with a death grip on his long hair, he still managed a couple of tricks before passing the ball to Moana. The crowd loved it.

Moana aimed for Rosie, but Councillor Bray intercepted with a header, which did serious damage to his comb-over. Both sides raced for the loose ball, then Liz broke free of the pack and, barely in control of the football, came flying down the field.

In goal, Kirsty screamed, "Lizzy, you're coming the wrong way!" Still running, Liz reached down to grab the ball then did a U-turn. Swerving around her bemused pursuers, she raced down the pitch and arms outstretched, threw herself across the goal line. "Try!" she yelled triumphantly. Everybody erupted into laughter.

Delores looked at Luke. "Should we allow that?"

"Of course." He looked at his mud-splattered wife, his friends, his kids and his community. And his heart swelled. "It was a home run."

Bundles of Joy—
coming next month to Superromance

Experience the romance, excitement and joy with 6 heartwarming titles.

BABY, I'M YOURS #1476 by *Carrie Weaver*

ANOTHER MAN'S BABY
(The Tulanes of Tennessee)
#1477 by *Kay Stockham*

THE MARINE'S BABY (9 Months Later)
#1478 by *Rogenna Brewer*

BE MY BABIES (Twins)
#1479 by *Kathryn Shay*

THE DIAPER DIARIES (Suddenly a Parent)
#1480 by *Abby Gaines*

HAVING JUSTIN'S BABY (A Little Secret)
#1481 by *Pamela Bauer*

Exciting, Emotional and Unexpected!

Look for these Superromance titles in March 2008.
Available wherever books are sold.

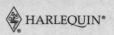

REQUEST YOUR FREE BOOKS!
2 FREE NOVELS PLUS 2 FREE GIFTS!

HARLEQUIN®

Super Romance®

Exciting, emotional, unexpected!

YES! Please send me 2 FREE Harlequin Superromance® novels and my 2 FREE gifts. After receiving them, if I don't wish to receive any more books, I can return the shipping statement marked "cancel." If I don't cancel, I will receive 6 brand-new novels every month and be billed just $4.69 per book in the U.S., or $5.24 per book in Canada, plus 25¢ shipping and handling per book and applicable taxes, if any*. That's a savings of close to 15% off the cover price! I understand that accepting the 2 free books and gifts places me under no obligation to buy anything. I can always return a shipment and cancel at any time. Even if I never buy another book from Harlequin, the two free books and gifts are mine to keep forever.

135 HDN EEX7   336 HDN EEYK

Name _____ (PLEASE PRINT) _____

Address _____ Apt. _____

City _____ State/Prov. _____ Zip/Postal Code _____

Signature (if under 18, a parent or guardian must sign)

Mail to the **Harlequin Reader Service®**:
IN U.S.A.: P.O. Box 1867, Buffalo, NY 14240-1867
IN CANADA: P.O. Box 609, Fort Erie, Ontario L2A 5X3

Not valid to current Harlequin Superromance subscribers.

Want to try two free books from another line?
Call 1-800-873-8635 or visit www.morefreebooks.com.

* Terms and prices subject to change without notice. NY residents add applicable sales tax. Canadian residents will be charged applicable provincial taxes and GST. This offer is limited to one order per household. All orders subject to approval. Credit or debit balances in a customer's account(s) may be offset by any other outstanding balance owed by or to the customer. Please allow 4 to 6 weeks for delivery.

Your Privacy: Harlequin is committed to protecting your privacy. Our Privacy Policy is available online at www.eHarlequin.com or upon request from the Reader Service. From time to time we make our lists of customers available to reputable firms who may have a product or service of interest to you. If you would prefer we not share your name and address, please check here. ☐

HSR07

HARLEQUIN® *Romance*®

MEDITERRANEAN
DADS

In the first of this emotional Mediterranean Dads duet,
nanny Julie is whisked away to a palatial Italian villa,
but she feels completely out of place in Massimo's
glamorous world. Her biggest challenge, though, is
ignoring her attraction to the brooding tycoon.

Look for

The Italian Tycoon
and the Nanny
by *Rebecca Winters*

in March wherever you buy books.

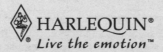

HARLEQUIN®
Live the emotion™

COMING NEXT MONTH

#1476 BABY, I'M YOURS · Carrie Weaver
As a recently widowed mom with three kids, Becca Smith struggles to keep life together. The discovery that she's pregnant is making things worse. There's only one person she can turn to—Rick Jensen. He's her business partner...and possibly this baby's father.

#1477 ANOTHER MAN'S BABY · Kay Stockham
The Tulanes of Tennessee
Landing in the ditch while in premature labor is not on Darcy Rhodes's to-do list. Fortunately, rescue arrives in the form of Garret Tulane. He seems so perfect, he's like Prince Charming. But will they forge their own happily ever after once the snow stops?

#1478 THE MARINE'S BABY · Rogenna Brewer
9 Months Later
Joining the military taught Lucky Calhoun the importance of family. And now he wants one of his own. That wish may come true sooner than planned. Thanks to a mix-up at the sperm bank, Caitlin Calhoun—his half brother's widow—seems to be carrying his child.

#1479 BE MY BABIES · Kathryn Shay
Twins
Simon McCarthy should not be attracted to Lily Wakefield. Not only is she new to town, but also she's pregnant—with twins. Still, the feelings between them make him think about their future together. Then her past catches up and threatens to destroy everything.

#1480 THE DIAPER DIARIES · Abby Gaines
Suddenly a Parent
A baby is so not playboy Tyler Warrington's thing. Still, he must care for the one who appeared on his doorstep. Fine. Hire a nanny. Then Bethany Hart talks her way into the job—for a cost. Funny, the more time he spends with her, the more willing he is to pay.

#1481 HAVING JUSTIN'S BABY · Pamela Bauer
Justin Collier has been Paige Stephens's best friend forever. Then one night she turns to him for comfort and...well, everything changes. Worse, she's now pregnant and he's proposing! She's always wanted to marry for love, but can Justin offer her that?

HSRCNM0208